"十三五"国家重点出版规划项目

李白诗歌全集英译
A Complete Edition of Pai Li's Poems in Chinese and English
With Annotations

赵彦春 译·注
Translated and Annotated by Yanchun Chao

第六卷
Volume VI

上海大学出版社
·上海·

卷 六

目　录
Contents

1221　**古近体诗三十三首**
　　　Old-new Rhythmic Poetry, 33 Poems

1223　送韩侍御之广德
　　　Seeing Off Han, the Royal Servant, to Broad Virtue

1224　送通禅师还南陵隐静寺
　　　Seeing Off T'ung, a Zen Master Back to Hidden Calm Temple at Southridge

1226　送友人
　　　Seeing Off a Friend

1227　送别
　　　Farewell

1228　江上送女道士褚三清游南岳
　　　Seeing Off Ch'u Three, a Woman Wordist, by a River to Tour Mt. Scale

1230　送友人入蜀
　　　Seeing Off a Friend to Shu

1231　送李青归华阳
　　　Seeing Off Ch'ing Li Back to Flowershine

1232　送舍弟
　　　Seeing Off My Brother

1233　送别
　　　Farewell

1234　送鞠十少府
　　　Seeing Off Chü Ten, the Royal Logistics Manager

1236 送张秀才谒高中丞
Seeing Off Chang, a Showcharm, to Pay His Respect to Governor Kao

1239 浔阳送弟昌峒鄱阳司马作
Seeing Off Ch'angtung, My Cousin in Bankshine to Serve P'oshine's Magistrate as an Assistant

1242 饯校书叔云
Giving a Farewell Dinner to Yün, My Uncle, a Collator

1244 送王孝廉觐省
Seeing Off Wang to See His Parents

1245 同吴王送杜秀芝赴举入京
Seeing Off Hsiuchih Tu with King of Wu to Capital for Grand Test

1247 洞庭醉后送绛州吕使君果流澧州
Seeing Off Kuo Lü, Prefect of Chiang Exiled to Sweetflow at Cavehall When I'm Drunk

1249 与诸公送陈郎将归衡阳
Seeing Off Langchiang Ch'en with My Friends Back to Scaleshine

1251 送赵判官赴黔府中丞叔幕
Seeing Off Chao, an Aide, to Serve in the Tent Office of His Uncle, Governor of Ch'ien

1254 送陆判官往琵琶峡
Seeing Off Lu, an Aide, to Lute Gorge

1255 送梁四归东平
Seeing Off Liang Four Back to East Peace

1257 江夏送友人
Seeing Off My Friend at Riversummer

1258 送郗昂谪巴中
Seeing Off Ang Ch'ieh Demoted to Pa

1259 江夏送张丞
Seeing Off Deputy Chang at Riversummer

1260 赋得白鹭鸶送宋少府入三峡
Following the Rhyme of Egrets Seeing Off Sung, the Royal Logistics Manager, to Three Gorges

1261	送二季之江东	
	Seeing Off My Two Cousins to East Land	
1263	江西送友人之罗浮	
	Seeing Off My Friend to Mt. La Phu	
1265	宣州谢朓楼饯别校书叔云	
	Seeing Off Yün, My Uncle, a Collator, on T'iao Hsieh's Tower in Hsuan	
1267	宣城送刘副使入秦	
	Seeing Off Vice Governor Liu to Ch'in at Hsuan	
1271	泾川送族弟錞	
	Seeing Off My Cousin Chun at the Ching Stream	
1274	五松山送殷淑	
	Seeing Off Shu Yin at Mt. Five Pines	
1276	送崔氏昆季之金陵	
	Seeing Off the K'un's Brothers to Gold Hill	
1278	登黄山凌歊台送族弟溧阳尉济充泛舟赴华阴	
	Climbing Mt. Yellow to Rising Mound, Boating with My Cousin Chich'ung, Sheriff of Lishine and Seeing Him Off to Flowershade	
1282	送储邕之武昌	
	Seeing Off Yung Ch'u to Mightboom	
1285	**古近体诗三十二首**	
	Old-new Rhythmic Poetry, 32 Poems	
1287	酬谈少府	
	A Talk with the Sheriff	
1289	酬宇文少府见赠桃竹书筒	
	Seeing Yüwen, the Royal Logistics Manager, Who Presents Me with the Peach Bamboo Canister	
1290	五月东鲁行答汶上君	
	A Reply to the Sneering Man on the Wen River on My Way to East Lu in the Fifth Moon	
1292	早秋单父南楼酬窦公衡	
	To Heng Tou in South Mansion in Shanfu on an Early Autumn Day	

1294 山中问答
Question and Answer in the Hills

1295 答友人赠乌纱帽
In Reply to My Friend's Gift of a Black Gauze Hat

1296 酬张司马赠墨
To Commander Chang, Who Gives Me Ink

1298 答湖州迦叶司马问白是何人
In Reply to Commander Kasyapa of Laketon, Who Asks Me Who I Am

1299 答长安崔少府叔封游终南翠微寺太宗皇帝金沙泉见寄
In Reply to Shufeng Ts'ui, Sheriff of Long Peace, Who Tours Emperor Grandsire's Sand Spring in Greenhill Temple in the South Mountains

1303 酬崔五郎中
To Ts'ui Five, the Royal Guard

1306 以诗代书答元丹丘
In Reply to Redknoll Yüan with a Verse Instead of a Letter

1308 金门答苏秀才
In Reply to Su, a Showcharm at Gold Gate

1312 酬坊州王司马与阎正字对雪见赠
In Reply to Commander Wang of Fangchow and Collator Yan, Facing Snow

1314 酬中都小吏携斗酒双鱼于逆旅见赠
To the Clerk from Mid-town, Who Gives Me Wine and Two Fish in an Inn

1316 酬张卿夜宿南陵见赠
In Reply to Shuming Chang Putting Up for the Night at Southridge

1319 酬岑勋见寻就元丹丘对酒相待以诗见招
To Hsun Tsen, Who Calls on Me, Talking About Redknoll Yüan's Treating Him with Wine and Verse

1322 答从弟幼成过西园见赠
In Reply to Yuch'eng, My Cousin, Who Calls on Me in West Garden

1324 酬王补阙惠翼庄庙宋丞泚赠别
Thanks to E Wang, the Remonstrant, and Tz'u Sung, the Manager of Huichuang Temple, Who Write Me Poems of Farewell

1327 酬裴侍御对雨感时见赠
In Reply to P'ei, the Royal Servant, Who Dedicates a Poem to Me While Viewing a Rain

1329 酬崔侍御
In Reply to Ts'ui, the Royal Servant

1330 玩月金陵城西孙楚酒楼,达曙歌吹,日晚乘醉著紫绮裘乌纱巾,与酒客数人棹歌秦淮,往石头访崔四侍御
Playing with the Crescent on Sun's Tower East of Gold Hill, Singing till Dawn and Rowing Drunk with a Few Drinkers in the Ch'inhuai River at Dusk in Purple Fur and Black Gauze Turban and Then Visiting Ts'ui, the Royal Servant, at Stone Town

1333 江上答崔宣城
In Reply to Ts'ui, Magistrate of Hsuan

1335 答族侄僧中孚赠玉泉仙人掌茶
In Reply to Chungfu, My Nephew, a Monk, Who Presents Me with Jade Spring Cactus Tea

1338 酬裴侍御留岫师弹琴见寄
In Reply to P'ei, the Royal Servant, Who Plays the Lute

1339 张相公出镇荆州,寻除太子詹事,余时流夜郎,行至江夏,与张公相去千里,公因太府丞王昔使车寄罗衣二事,及五月五日赠余诗,余答以此诗
Chang, the Scholar, Is Appointed as Prefect of Chaste and Before Long Becomes Chief Supervisor of Crown Prince When I Reach Riversummer on My Way to Exile in Nightboy, a Thousand *Li* from Premier Chang and I Present This Verse to Him on the Fifth Day of the Fifth Moon to Express My Gratitude for His Sending Me a Silk Gown Together with a Verse by a Cart Sent by Hsi Wang, a Grand Hall Manager

1341 醉后答丁十八以诗讥余捶碎黄鹤楼
In Reply to Ting Eighteen, Who Sneers at Me, Accusing Me of Smashing Yellow Crane Tower When I'm Drunk

1343 答裴侍御先行至石头驿以书见招,期月满泛洞庭
In Reply to P'ei, the Royal Servant, Who Arrives at Stone Station and Writes Me an Invitation to Boating on Lake Cavehall on a Full Moon

1345	答高山人兼呈权顾二侯	
	In Reply to Kao, the Hermit, and Also to Ch'üan and Ku	
1349	答杜秀才五松见赠	
	In Reply to Tu, the Showcharm Who Writes Me a Poem at Mt. Five Pines	
1354	至陵阳山登天柱石酬韩侍御见招隐黄山	
	Climbing Heavenly Crag on Mt. Ridgeshine to Thank Han, the Royal Servant, Who Has Invited Me to Mt. Yellow	
1358	酬崔十五见招	
	To Ts'ui Fifteen, Who Gives Me a Treat	
1359	答王十二寒夜独酌有怀	
	In Reply to Wang Twelve, Who Drinks Alone at Night	

1365 古近体诗六十首
Old-new Rhythmic Poetry, 60 Poems

1367	游南阳白水登石激作	
	Touring White Water Source in Southshine	
1368	游南阳清泠泉	
	Touring the Cold Spring in Southshine	
1369	寻鲁城北范居士失道落苍耳中见范置酒摘苍耳作	
	On My Way to Visit Fan, the Hermit, I Go Astray and Fall into Cocklebur and Then I Meet with Him, Who Treats Me with Wine and Picks Cocklebur off Me	
1372	东鲁门泛舟二首	
	Boating at Gate of East Lu, Two Poems	
1374	秋猎孟诸夜归置酒单父东楼观妓	
	Returning at Night from Autumn Hunting at Mengchu and Watching Singing Girls at Feast on East Tower in Shanfu	
1376	游泰山六首	
	Touring Mt. Arch, Six Poems	
1389	秋夜与刘砀山泛宴喜亭池	
	Attending a Feast with Fan Liu, Magistrate of Tangshan, at Glee Kiosk Pool on an Autumn Night	

1391	携妓登梁王栖霞山孟氏桃园中 Climbing Mt. Perching Clouds of Prince Liang with Courtesans and Entering Meng's Peach Orchard
1393	与从侄杭州刺史良游天竺寺 Touring Heaven Bamboo Temple with Liang, My Cousin, Governor of Hangchow
1395	同友人舟行游台越作 Cruising T'aiyüeh with My Friend
1397	下终南山过斛斯山人宿置酒 Descending the South Mountains to Drink with Ssu Hu, a Hermit
1399	朝下过卢郎中叙旧游 A Talk of the Past with Lu, the Royal Guard, After the Levee
1401	侍从游宿温泉宫作 Escorting the Lord to Hot Spring Palace
1402	邯郸南亭观妓 Watching Playgirls at South Pavilion in Hantan
1404	春日游罗敷潭 Touring La Phu Abyss on a Spring Day
1405	春陪商州裴使君游石娥溪 Accompanying Lord P'ei, a Civil Governor from Shangchow on a Tour to the Stone Maid Stream
1408	陪从祖济南太守泛鹊山湖三首 Accompanying My Granduncle, Magistrate of Chinan, Boating on Lake Magpie, Three Poems
1411	春日陪杨江宁及诸官宴北湖感古作 Accompanying Magistrate Yang of Riverpeace and Other Officials at Feast on North Lake While Reminiscing the Past
1414	宴郑参卿山池 Inviting Cheng, Chief of Staff, to a Feast
1415	游谢氏山亭 Touring Hsieh's Pavilion
1417	把酒问月 Asking the Moon, Cup in Hand

1419 同族侄评事黯游昌禅师山池二首
Touring a Zen Master's Mountain Pool with My Nephew, An, a Reviewer, Two Poems

1422 金陵凤凰台置酒
Drinking on Phoenix Mound in Gold Hill

1424 秋浦清溪雪夜对酒，客有唱山鹧鸪者
Drinking Wine at Clear Creek in Autumn Shore on a Snowy Night, When a Guest Sings *Partridge*

1426 与周刚清溪玉镜潭宴别
A Farewell Party for Kang Chou at Jade Mirror Pool in the Clear Stream

1429 游秋浦白笴陂二首
Touring White Arrow Slope in Autumn Shore, Two Poems

1431 宴陶家亭子
A Feast at the T'ao's Pavilion

1432 在水军宴韦司马楼船观妓
Watching Courtesans Dancing at a Feast in a Tower Ship of the Navy Under General Wei

1433 流夜郎至江夏，陪长史叔及薛明府宴兴德寺南阁
Accompanying My Uncle, Vice Inspector, and Magistrate Hsüeh at Feast in the Southern Hall of Virtue Raising Temple at Riversummer on My Way to Nightboy When I Am Exiled

1435 泛沔州城南郎官湖
Boating on Officials Lake South of Mien Town

1437 陪侍郎叔游洞庭醉后三首
Accompanying My Uncle, a Vice Minister, on a Visit to Lake Cavehall, After Being Drunk, Three Poems

1440 夜泛洞庭，寻裴侍御清酌
Rowing on Lake Cavehall to Find P'ei, the Royal Servant, for a Drink

1442 陪族叔刑部侍郎晔及中书贾舍人至游洞庭五首
Accompanying My Uncle, Yeh, Minister of Penalty, and Chih Chia, Scribe of Privy Council on Lake Cavehall, Five Poems

1447	楚江黄龙矶南宴杨执戟治楼 Feasting with Yang South of Yellow Dragon Rocks near the Ch'u River	
1449	铜官山醉后绝句 A Quatrain After I'm Drunk at the Copper Hills	
1450	与南陵常赞府游五松山 Touring Mt. Five Pines with Ch'ang, Magistrate of Southridge	
1452	宣城青溪 The Clear Brook in Hsuan	
1453	与谢良辅游泾川陵岩寺 Visiting Rock Temple by the Ching Stream with Liangfu Hsieh	
1454	游水西简郑明府 Touring West Water to See Magistrate Cheng	
1456	九日登山 Climbing a Mountain on Double Ninth Day	
1459	九日 The Ninth Day	
1461	九日龙山饮 Drinking on Mt. Dragon the Ninth Day	
1462	九月十日即事 The Tenth Day of the Ninth Moon, an Observation	
1463	陪族叔当涂宰游化城寺升公清风亭 Accompanying My Uncle, Magistrate of Tangt'u, Visiting Breeze Arbor at Transmigration Temple	

古近体诗三十三首
Old-new Rhythmic Poetry, 33 Poems

送韩侍御之广德

昔日绣衣何足荣，
今宵贳酒与君倾。
暂就东山赊月色，
酣歌一夜送泉明。

Seeing Off Han, the Royal Servant, to Broad Virtue

How glorious I felt for my brocade before;
Today I'll borrow wine for you, let's drink more.
East Hills, can you lend me moonlight, pure light?
We will sing all night to the fountain bright.

* Broad Virtue: Broad Virtue County in the northeast of today's Anhui Province.
* East Hills: the East Hills, located in Shaohsing, a place for reclusion, where Steady Stone, that is, An Hsieh (A.D. 320 - A.D. 385) used to live.
* the fountain bright: the pool bright. As Emperor Highsire of T'ang was Pool Li by name, the word pool was a taboo in the T'ang dynasty, so when our poet used "fountain", he actullay meant "pool". "The fountain bright" implies Poolbright T'ao, the famous poet and hermit in the Southern Sung dynasty or his hermitage.

送通禅师还南陵隐静寺

我闻隐静寺，
山水多奇踪。
岩种朗公橘，
门深杯渡松。
道人制猛虎，
振锡还孤峰。
他日南陵下，
相期谷口逢。

Seeing Off T'ung, a Zen Master Back to Hidden Calm Temple at Southridge

The Hidden Calm Temple, I hear,
Sees many hills and rills so queer.
On the rocks Lang's tangerines grow;
Behind the gate Cup Float Pines show.
A Wordist does a tiger kill;
A monk will climb a lonely hill.
When you come to Southridge some day,
Meet in front of the dale we may.

* Zen Master: an honored master who practices Zen, a kind of performance of quietude in a form of meditation or contemplation. When Sanskrit jana was spread to China, it was translated as Zan or Zen for this kind of practice. In the T'ang dynasty, Zen had become very influential among the intellectuals, many of whom were associated with Zen monks and spent time in Zen monasteries.
* the Hidden Calm Temple: a temple 10 kilometers from Prosper (Fanch'ang) County in

today's Anhui Province.
* Lang's tangerines: unidentified.
* Cup Float Pines: pines planted by Cup Float, a monk in the Chin and Southern Sung dynasties.
* Wordist: a follower or practitioner of Wordism.
* tiger: a large carnivorous feline mammal of Asia, with vertical black wavy stripes on a tawny body and black bars or rings on the limbs and tail, praised as king of all animals.
* Southridge: a county in the southeast of today's Anhui Province.

送　友　人

青山横北郭，
白水绕东城。
此地一为别，
孤蓬万里征。
浮云游子意，
落日故人情。
挥手自兹去，
萧萧班马鸣。

Seeing Off a Friend

Green mountains stand by the north end;
White waters run east of the town.
Now you're leaving, my heart does rend;
You're drifting off like a blown down.
The hanging clouds would linger high;
The sinking sun would up there stay.
Raising our hands, we wave good bye;
Our steeds, apart now, loudly neigh.

* Our steeds, apart now, loudly neigh: even the horses are reluctant to go apart, an allusion to *Chariot Strong* from *The Book of Songs* compiled by Confucius 2,500 years ago: "Long, long the horses neigh; / Standards and banners wave. / The kitchen won't full stay / If the hunters aren't brave."

送　别

斗酒渭城边，
垆头醉不眠。
梨花千树雪，
杨叶万条烟。
惜别倾壶醑，
临分赠马鞭。
看君颍上去，
新月到应圆。

Farewell

Out of Wei Town we drink wine deep;
Drunk in the wine shop, we can't sleep.
A thousand pear blooms are white snow;
A million poplar leaves in mist flow.
Just drink more wine before you go;
If you start, I've this whip for you.
For the Ying River you're now bound;
When you arrive, the moon is round.

* Wei Town: what was Allshine County in Ch'in, Wei County in Han, now a district of Allshine.
* poplar: any of a genus (*Populus*) of dioecious trees and bushes of the willow family, widely distributed in the northern hemisphere.
* the Ying River: a river derived from Mt. Tower, the biggest branch of the Huai River. The River Ying has been regarded as one of the origins of Chinese culture.
* the moon: the celestial body that revolves around the earth from west to east, which appears at night and gives off shining silvery light, an image of purity and solitude and reunion when round in Chinese culture.

江上送女道士褚三清游南岳

吴江女道士，
头戴莲花巾。
霓衣不湿雨，
特异阳台神。
足下远游履，
凌波生素尘。
寻仙向南岳，
应见魏夫人。

Seeing Off Ch'u Three, a Woman Wordist, by a River to Tour Mt. Scale

A woman Wordist's in Wu there;
A lotus bloom scarf she does wear.
Her clothes not wet in rain as found,
Different that of Nymph on Sun Mound.
She tours, wearing long journey shoes;
Green waves rush while ahead she goes.
If you climb Scale to seek a fay,
Perhaps you will find Lady Way.

* Wordist: one who believes in or professes belief of Wordism, the doctrines declared by Laocius (571 B.C.- 471 B.C.).
* Wu: the State of Wu or a southern area.
* Nymph: referring to Goddess of Mt. Witch, a beautiful fairy dwelling in Mt. Witch, who shaped herself as clouds at dawn and turned into rain at dusk. In myths, King Huai of Ch'u once met her in his dream, and had an intercourse overnight. The story was

recorded by Jade Sung, a student of Yüan Ch'ü's, when he travelled to Cloud Dream Moor with King Hsiang.

* Sun Mound: where Goddess of Mt. Witch dated with King Hsiang of Ch'u.
* Scale: Mt. Scale, one of the Five Mountains in China, located in Hunan Province, along with Mt. Ever in Shanhsi, Mt. Arch in Shantung, Mt. Flora in Sha'anhsi, and Mt. Tower in Honan.
* Lady Way: a highborn lady, keen on the Word and had been cultivating herself throughout her life. At the age of 83, an immortal came to pick her up to Heaven and made her a patron of Mt. Scale.

送友人入蜀

见说蚕丛路，
崎岖不易行。
山从人面起，
云傍马头生。
芳树笼秦栈，
春流绕蜀城。
升沉应已定，
不必问君平。

Seeing Off a Friend to Shu

To wend to Shu, as people say,
It's hard, a zigzag, zigzag way.
Crags in front of your face arise,
And clouds assault your horse's eyes.
Trees shade the cliff trail up and down;
Spring streams gurgle around the town.
Your fate has been arranged indeed;
To ask a wizard there's no need.

* Shu: one of the earliest kingdoms in China, founded by Silkworm according to legend. In the Three Kingdoms period, a new Shu was established by Pei Liu, hence one of the three kingdoms in that period.
* to ask a wizard: an allusion to Chünp'ing Yan, a fortune teller in Silkton (Ch'engtu) under the Han dynasty. As soon as he had earned enough for a living, he would close his shop and busy himself writing books.

送李青归华阳

伯阳仙家子，
容色如青春。
日月秘灵洞，
云霞辞世人。
化心养精魄，
隐几窅天真。
莫作千年别，
归来城郭新。

Seeing Off Ch'ing Li Back to Flowershine

You are Bigshine, the hermit's son;
Like a spring bloom your face does shine.
In Soul Cave you hide moon and sun;
The dusty world you now decline.
Your solitude your essence rears;
And your calmness keeps what is true.
Don't stay there for one thousand years;
When back, you'll find the town turn new.

* Flowershine: referring to an area in the southern side of the Ch'in Ridge.
* Bigshine: referring to Laocius, surnamed Li, styled Ear and dubbed Bigshine, from the State of Ch'en (1046 B.C.- 478 B.C.), born in the Shang dynasty (1600 B.C.- cir. 1046 B.C.) as one source says. He was an undercolumn historian, then an archive historian in the Chough dynasty (1046 B.C.- 256 B.C.), a position he served for more than eighty years (more than two hundred years according to *Historical Records*).
* Soul Cave: a cave for fairies, location unidentified.

送 舍 弟

吾家白额驹,
远别临东道。
他日相思一梦君,
应得池塘生春草。

Seeing Off My Brother

O brother, you're a pony white;
On East Road here, we part, alas.
Maybe, I'll dream of you some day, some night;
The pond there should be so lush with spring grass.

送　别

水色南天远，
舟行若在虚。
迁人发佳兴，
吾子访闲居。
日落看归鸟，
潭澄羡跃鱼。
圣朝思贾谊，
应降紫泥书。

Farewell

The water rolls to the far blue;
It seems the boat thru void does row.
Tho exilcd, you have the very zest
And have come to where I now rest.
The setting sun sees birds home fly;
The limpid pond views fish leap spry.
For an Ee Chia the Lord does look,
He'd send you a Sealed Purple Book.

* Sealed Purple Book: referring to an imperial edict. Ancient Chinese would envelop their letter with clay and impress it with a seal while an edict would be enveloped with purple clay, hence the name of Sealed Purple Book.
* Ee Chia: Ee Chia (200 B.C.- 168 B.C.), a political commentator, litterateur, who gained his fame as a talented youth. When he served as an official, he was envied by those higher-ranking ministers. In 176 B.C., Chia was demoted and dispatched to Long Sand as Teacher of the Prince of Long Sand. Three years later, he was called back to Long Peace and died at 33.

送鞠十少府

试发清秋兴，
因为吴会吟。
碧云敛海色，
流水折江心。
我有延陵剑，
君无陆贾金。
艰难此为别，
惆怅一何深。

Seeing Off Chü Ten, the Royal Logistics Manager

I'm up as autumn now does come,
Therefore a southern song I hum.
The clouds do dim the ocean hue;
A whirlpool follows the sea flow.
Prince Yanling's sword I have in vain;
No Lu's monies with you remain.
In here it's hard to say good-bye;
How deeply I release a sigh.

* Prince Yanling: referring to Stripfour (576 B.C.- 484 B.C.), Chi Cha if transliterated, who declined the throne and farmed in Broadridge. Stripfour was an honest and righteous man. When Stripfour traveled to the State of Hsu, the lord of the state liked his sword but was reluctant to ask. Stripfour did not give the sword because his journey had not been finished. When Stripfour came back, he found the lord had already passed away, so Stripfour left his sword at the tomb to keep his promise he made in his

heart.
* Lu's monies: the monies made and saved while in an official post. Chia Lu (cir. 240 B.C.-170 B.C.), the great thinker in the Western Han dynasty divided his savings into five portions equally for his five sons as their principal input.

送张秀才谒高中丞

秦帝沦玉镜,
留侯降氛氲。
感激黄石老,
经过沧海君。
壮士挥金槌,
报仇六国闻。
智勇冠终古,
萧陈难与群。
两龙争斗时,
天地动风云。
酒酣舞长剑,
仓卒解汉纷。
宇宙初倒悬,
鸿沟势将分。
英谋信奇绝,
夫子扬清芬。
胡月入紫微,
三光乱天文。
高公镇淮海,
谈笑却妖氛。
采尔幕中画,
戡难光殊勋。
我无燕霜感,
玉石俱烧焚。
但洒一行泪,
临歧竟何云。

Seeing Off Chang, a Showcharm, to Pay His Respect to Governor Kao

Then Emperor Ch'in lost the Way,
And Liang Chang would this tyrant slay.
Thanks to Yellow Stone, the old man,
He did this assassin well train.
This brave man swayed his hammer gold;
His tale in Six States has been told.
His courage and wits last for e'er,
E'en Hsiao and Ch'en could not compare.
And then two dragons fought a war,
Wherefrom did wind sough and clouds soar.
At feast, a long sword Kuai Fan waved,
Hence from a tangle Liu was saved.
Then the cosmos turned upside down;
The trench the other side would drown.
Liang Chang's resourcefulness became
Well known, and hence Yellow Stone's fame.
The Hun man would the throne o'erthrow;
The riot of Three Lights dimmed the glow.
Kao garrisoned the Huai and Sea,
And wiped the rebels all with glee.
Your strategy was well received;
A great success you then achieved.
Not wronged I felt, not wronged at all;
With burned stone, jade may often fall.
At crisis what more should I say?
My strings of tears speak their own way.

* showcharm: a talent recommended for official use through imperial civil-service examinations or a well-learned person in ancient China.
* Hsiao: referring to Ho Hsiao (257 B.C.- 193 B.C.), a statesman, the first prime minister and one of the Three Standouts in the early Han dynasty.
* Ch'en: referring to P'ing Ch'en, a minister in the Western Han dynasty.
* two dragons: referring to Yü Hsiang (232 B.C.- 202 B.C.), Overlord of West Ch'u, and Pang Liu (256 B.C - 195 B.C.), Lord Highsire of Han, the founding lord of the Western Han dynasty.
* Kuai Fan: Kuai Fan (242 B.C.- 189 B.C.), a founding commander of Han. When the Han group went to the Swangate banquet, Liang Chang asked Kuai Fan to wave his sword to protect Pang Liu, which helped their lord out of the crisis.
* cosmos: the world or universe considered as a system, perfect in order and arrangement, opposed to chaos.
* Liu: referring to Pang Liu, the founding emperor of Han.
* Liang Chang: Liang Chang (250 B.C.- 186 B.C.), a renowned strategist in Chinese history and one of the Three Standouts of the early Han. When people suffered from Emperor First's tyranny, Liang Chang hired a strong man to assassinate the emperor with a golden hammer. After the failed assassination, he escaped and met Yellow Stone. Polite and respectful, he won the legendary Wordist Yellow Stone's trust and received *The Art of War* from him. By studying the book, Liang Chang became a wise and resourceful brain truster. After the reign of Han was stabilized, he asked for retirement and followed Red Pine to be an immortal. The poet takes Liang Chang as a symbolic figure of his own to imply his hidden talent and ambition.
* Yellow Stone: the Wordist who gave Liang Chang *The Art of War*.
* Three Lights: referring to the sun, the moon, and stars. Sir Lush mentioned Three Lights describing the sword of vassal lords in *Loving Swords* from *Sir Lush*: "Above, it is modeled on Heaven, answering to the sun, the moon, and the stars; below, it is based on the earth, agreeing to the four seasons; in the middle, it responds to the people's will and pacifies the four directions."
* Kao: referring to Shi Kao (A.D. 704 - A.D. 765), a commander and fortress poet of T'ang.

浔阳送弟昌峒鄱阳司马作

桑落洲渚连，
沧江无云烟。
寻阳非剡水，
忽见子猷船。
飘然欲相近，
来迟杳若仙。
人乘海上月，
帆落湖中天。
一睹无二诺，
朝欢更胜昨。
尔则吾惠连，
吾非尔康乐。
朱绂白银章，
上官佐鄱阳。
松门拂中道，
石镜回清光。
摇扇及于越，
水亭风气凉。
与尔期此亭，
期在秋月满。
时过或未来，
两乡心已断。
吴山对楚岸，
彭蠡当中州。
相思定如此，
有穷尽年愁。

Seeing Off Ch'angtung, My Cousin in Bankshine to Serve P'oshine's Magistrate as an Assistant

There on the shoals mulberries fall;
The Dark Blue has no mist at all.
The Bankshine is not the Yan, no!
Lo, Tsuyu's boat, it does here flow.
It floats on and on, near and near,
Much like a fairy does appear.
The moon at sea one may go take;
The sail falls to the clouded lake.
Our promise we keep, we keep fast;
Today we're happier than the past.
You're my cousin so dear indeed,
I'm not your brother as you need.
O red band and silver badge, great,
You're but to help P'oshine's magistrate.
Pine trees at the gate shade the way;
The Stone Mirror shines, a bright ray.
When in Yüeh with the fan you hold,
To the kiosk will blow a wind cold.
Let me meet you in the kiosk there,
With the moon shining, round and fair.
If for too long we stay apart,
So far off, we may lose our heart.
The Wu hills do the Ch'u bank see;
In Lake P'oshine a shoal there be.
I think I would be helpless here,

So wretched and sad all the year.

* the Bankshine: the Nine, a group of nine rivers while Bankshine is an ancient name of present-day Chiuchiang, Chianghsi Province.
* P'oshine: referring to P'oyang if transliterated, a county in present-day Chianghsi.
* the Yan: the Yan River, originating from Mt. Fourbright, 98 kilometers long with a drainage area of 2,223 square kilometers.
* Tsuyu: referring to Huichih Wang (A.D. 338 – A.D. 386), a renowned calligrapher with a carefree attitude in the Eastern Chin dynasty, Tsu-yu by courtesy name. He once took a boat to visit his friend on a whim on a winter evening, and returned without seeing him. All the same, Hui already felt contented on the way.
* the moon: the planet of the earth, which appears at night and gives off shining silvery light, an image of purity and solitude in Chinese culture.
* Yüeh: referring to the eastern lands where the State of Yüeh was located.
* Lake P'oshine: the biggest freshwater lake in China, located in Chianghsi.

饯校书叔云

少年费白日，
歌笑矜朱颜。
不知忽已老，
喜见春风还。
惜别且为欢，
徘徊桃李间。
看花饮美酒，
听鸟临晴山。
向晚竹林寂，
无人空闭关。

Giving a Farewell Dinner to Yün, My Uncle, a Collator

When young I wasted so much time,
Mad, glad as if I'd stay in prime.
I have grown old fast unawares;
Now you come here, back are spring airs.
We'll soon part, do drink to our mood,
And let's stroll now in the peach wood.
Let's view the flowers, a-drinking wine
And hear birds flying to Mt. Shine.
The dusk has calmed the bamboo grove;
It seems closed as no people rove.

* peach: any of the plant (*Prunus Percica*), bearing a fleshy, juicy, edible drupe, cultivated in many varieties in temperate zones considered sacred in China, often used as a metaphor for a young woman, as a section of a poem in *The Book of Songs* reads: The peach twigs sway, / Ablaze the flower; / Now she's married away, / Befitting her new bower.

* Mt. Shine: unidentified in this poem, probably a sunlit peak.
* the bamboo grove: an allusion to the place the talented Seven Sages in the Chin dynasty gathered, drinking and merry making.

送王孝廉觐省

彭蠡将天合,
姑苏在日边。
宁亲候海色,
欲动孝廉船。
窈窕晴江转,
参差远岫连。
相思无昼夜,
东注似长川。

Seeing Off Wang to See His Parents

Lake P'oshine merges with the skies;
Kusu is where the sun does rise.
You wait till it's right time to go;
To see your parents you will row.
The stream reflects as it is fine;
The hills afar roll to combine.
We'll miss each other night and day,
Like the Long pours east all the way.

* Lake P'oshine: the biggest freshwater lake in China, located in Chianghsi.
* Kusu: an alternative name for Soochow, the capital of Wu, an important city of today's Chiangsu Province. Aged 2,500, it is the birth place of Wu culture, eulogized as Heaven on Earth and Eastern Venice, bristled with waterways, gardens and pagodas.
* the Long: the longest river in China, regarded as Mother of Chinese culture, originating from the T'angkula Mountains on Tibet Plateau, flowing through 11 provincial areas, more than 6,300 kilometers long, the third longest river in the world.

同吴王送杜秀芝赴举入京

秀才何翩翩，
王许回也贤。
暂别庐江守，
将游京兆天。
秋山宜落日，
秀水出寒烟。
欲折一枝桂，
还来雁沼前。

Seeing Off Hsiuchih Tu with King of Wu to Capital for Grand Test

How brilliant! What a man, what grace!
Your sainthood King of Wu does praise.
Now leaving Magistrate of Lu,
Capital you're going to view.
The autumn hills touched with sun rays,
The water blue's veiled with cold haze.
May you pick up the laurel spray
So we will drink for your good day.

* Grand Test: referring to imperial civil-service examinations for selecting talents to serve as governmental officials, a system and practice initiated in the Han dynasty (202 B.C.-A.D. 220), formally begun in the Sui dynasty (A.D. 581 - A.D. 619), well-developed in the T'ang dynasty (A.D. 618 - A.D. 907) and abolished in the Late Ch'ing dynasty (A.D. 1636 - A.D. 1912).
* your sainthood: alluding to Hui Yan (521 B.C.- 481 B.C.) or Yanhui, Confucius' most

diligent student, the first of Confucius's seventy-two well-established disciples, and a thinker in the late Spring and Autumn period. Confucius once commended him like this:"What a man Yanhui is! With a bowl of meal, a kettle of water, he lives in a shabby hut. No one can tolerate such poverty, but Yanhui feels happy about it. What a man he is!"

* Wu: a southern vassal state of Chough, founded by Usetwo, King Civil of Chough' uncle in the early years of Chough, and subjugated and annexed by the State of Yüeh in 437 B.C.
* Lu: referring to Lodge, present-day Hofei, the capital of Anhui Province.
* Caiptal: referring to Long Peace or Ch'ang'an if transliterated, the capital of the T'ang Empire, with 1,000,000 inhabitants, the largest walled city ever built by man, and a cosmopolis swarming with all dignitaries from the world and the center of world religions, Buddhism, Confucianism, Wordism, Nestorianism, Zoroastrianism, and even Islamism represented by Saracens. Having evolved through the ages of Chough, Ch'in, Chin, Western Way, Later Chough, Sui and T'ang, it is now Hsi-an, West Peace literally, the capital of Sha'anhsi Province.

洞庭醉后送绛州吕使君果流澧州

昔别若梦中，
天涯忽相逢。
洞庭破秋月，
纵酒开愁容。
赠剑刻玉字，
延平两蛟龙。
送君不尽意，
书及雁回峰。

Seeing Off Kuo Lü, Prefect of Chiang Exiled to Sweetflow at Cavehall When I'm Drunk

Our farewell's just like yesterday;
As vagrants we meet on our way.
On Lake Cavehall amid moonshine,
Let's cheer up, so given to wine.
I will give you my inscribed sword,
With dragons two from Yanp'ing Ford.
I can't be well expressed, alack;
I'll write to you at Wild Geese Back.

* Lake Cavehall: a large lake in today's Hunan Province.
* dragons two from Yanp'ing Ford: referring to two renowned ancient swords—Kanchiang and Moyeh. They were once collected by Huan Lei in the West Chin dynasty. He gave Kanchiang to his friend Hua Chang and kept Moyeh. But Kanchiang

was lost after Chang was murdered. After Lei's death, when his son Hua Lei passed by Yanp'ing Ford, all of a sudden, Moyeh jumped off his waist to the water to join its partner Kanchiang, and the two swords turned into two dragons.

* Wild Geese Back: a peak in the south of Scaleshine. Ancients believed that it was the extreme south that wild geese would fly to.

与诸公送陈郎将归衡阳

衡山苍苍入紫冥，
下看南极老人星。
回飙吹散五峰雪，
往往飞花落洞庭。
气清岳秀有如此，
郎将一家拖金紫。
门前食客乱浮云，
世人皆比孟尝君。
江上送行无白璧，
临歧惆怅若为分。

Seeing Off Langchiang Ch'en with My Friends Back to Scaleshine

Mt. Scale dark green blends with the nightly skies;
Down looking, one sees Old Man Star south rise
A blizzard from the five peaks whirls up snow,
Which, blossom-like, falls to Cavehall below.
The mounts look beautiful in such pure air;
Ch'en's whole family do gold armors wear.
Hangers-on like clouds float, many and more;
All compare him to Lord of Mengch'ang of yore.
No white waves rush over to our good-bye;
Now you depart, divided is our sigh.

* Scaleshine: referring to Hengyang if transliterated, a city in present-day Hunan

Province.
* Mt. Scale: one of the Five Mountains in China, located in Hunan Province, along with Mt. Ever in Shanhsi, Mt. Arch in Shantung, Mt. Flora in Sha'anhsi, and Mt. Tower in Honan.
* Old Man Star: *Polaris Australis*, the star over South Pole, visible to the naked eye, regarded as the star of longevity in olden times, used as a eulogy for an elder on the occasion of his birthday celebration.
* Cavehall: a large lake in approximately today's Hunan Province.
* Mengch'ang: Lord of Mengch'ang of Ch'i, one of the Four Gallants in the Warring States period.

送赵判官赴黔府中丞叔幕

廓落青云心，
结交黄金尽。
富贵翻相忘，
令人忽自哂。
蹭蹬鬓毛斑，
盛时难再还。
巨源咄石生，
何事马蹄间？
绿萝长不厌，
却欲还东山。
君为鲁曾子，
拜揖高堂里。
叔继赵平原，
偏承明主恩。
风霜推独坐，
旌节镇雄藩。
虎士秉金钺，
蛾眉开玉樽。
才高幕下去，
义重林中言。
水宿五溪月，
霜啼三峡猿。
东风春草绿，
江上候归轩。

Seeing Off Chao, an Aide, to Serve in the Tent Office of His Uncle, Governor of Ch'ien

In vain a climbing heart I hold;
In dealings I've spent all my gold.
Once one's rich, he forgets you sheer;
You cannot but to yourself sneer.
Now with gray hair I'm old and slack;
Once prime is gone, it can't come back.
Once T'ao Shan to Chien Shih did shout:
What are you so busy about?
Of trailers green I never tire;
To go back east I much desire.
With Tsengcius' kindness, kindness enow,
To your parents you keenly bow.
Your uncle like Prince of Chao then
Is His Majesty's favored man.
He sits sedate with wind and frost,
And guards the fronts not to be crossed.
His soldiers brave halberds hold up;
His singer cute drinks him a cup.
Now you're to serve him in his tent,
Devout and on loyalty bent.
You'll live on the moonlit Fifth Stream,
And at Three Gorges hear apes scream.
When east wind blows a green spring tide,
For boat thine I'll wait riverside.

* Ch'ien: an alternative name for Kuichow.
* T'ao Shan: one of the Seven Sages of Bamboo Groves in the Chin dynasty. T'ao Shan saw through Ssuma Ee's plan, so he woke Chien Shih up at night and urged him to think about it. But Chien Shih did not care. T'ao Shan, then, shouted to him, hoping him would not be busy with warfare. Not long after, Ssuma Ee started a fight.
* Chien Shih: Chien Shih (? - A.D. 350), a lord of Later Chao in the Sixteen States period.
* Tsengcius: Tsengcius (505 B. C. - 435 B. C.), Confucius's student, one of the representatives of Confucianism, the author of *The Book of Filial Piety*.
* Prince of Chao: referring to Lord Plain of Chao, one of the Four Childes in the Warring States Period who was generous and noble enough to attract many hangers-on to his house.
* The Fifth Stream: there were five streams in Ch'ien, the fifth one is the Juan Stream.
* Three Gorges: referring to the three gorges of the Long River, including Big Pond Gorge, Witch Gorge, and Westridge Gorge, a set of spectacular gorges formed where the Long River cuts its way through the formidable Witch Mountains, forming a three-hundred-kilometer stretch of very narrow canyons.

送陆判官往琵琶峡

水国秋风夜，
殊非远别时。
长安如梦里，
何日是归期。

Seeing Off Lu, an Aide, to Lute Gorge

The wetland night, an autumn blow,
Now at this time, you shouldn't go.
Long Peace does in my dream appear;
When will you come back to me here?

* Lute Gorge: below Mt. Witch, looking like a lute.
* Long Peace: referring to Ch'ang'an if transliterated, the capital of the T'ang, at which time it boasted a population of million, the largest walled city ever built by man, and a cosmopolis of world religions, Buddhism, Confucianism, Wordism, Nestorianism, Zoroastrianism, and even Islamism represented by Saracens. It was the wonder of the age that reached the pinnacle of brilliance in Emperor Deepsire's reign: The main castle with its nine-fold gates, the thirty-six imperial palaces, pillars of gold, innumerable mansions and villas of noblemen, the broad avenues thronged with motley crowds of townsfolk, gallants on horseback, and mandarin cars drawn by yokes of black oxen, countless houses of pleasure, which opened their doors by night all made this city a kaleidoscope of miracles.

送梁四归东平

玉壶契美酒，
送别强为欢。
大火南星月，
长郊北路难。
殷王期负鼎，
汶水起垂竿。
莫学东山卧，
参差老谢安。

Seeing Off Liang Four Back to East Peace

The jade pot full of farewell wine;
I forced a smile to say: It's fine.
It's so hot, a mid-summer's day;
To go north, it'll be a hard way.
King of Shang longed for talents great.
Pack up your fishing rod and bait.
Don't, like Hsieh, in the East Hills lie;
Your prime will age as time goes by.

* jade pot: a pot in good quality, crystally bright, usually alluding to the purity of the holder's heart.
* King of Shang: Hotspring of Shang (cir. 1670 B.C.- 1587 B.C.), the founding king of Shang, who annihilated Hsia with the help of two talents Yin Ee and Chunghui as his two prime ministers.
* Hsieh: referring to An Hsieh (A.D. 320 - A.D. 385), a statesman and renowned

scholar in the Eastern Chin dynasty. He once lived in seclusion and went back to defend the country when Chien Fu sent troops to conquer Eastern Chin.

* the East Hills: a place for reclusion, located in today's Shaohsing, Chechiang Province, the hills where An Hsieh (A.D. 320 – A.D. 385), a statesman and litterateur with high reputation, lived with ease and kept declining official positions until he was in his forties. It is often used as a metaphor for reclusion.

江夏送友人

雪点翠云裘，
送君黄鹤楼。
黄鹤振玉羽，
西飞帝王州。
凤无琅玕实，
何以赠远游？
徘徊相顾影，
泪下汉江流。

Seeing Off My Friend at Riversummer

Your fur coat is dotted with snow;
Yellow Crane Tower now sees you go.
The yellow crane spreads wings on high;
To Capital west it will fly.
A phoenix, I've no food with me;
You're going, what shall I give thee?
While at my shadow I look back,
My tears drop to the stream, alack.

* Riversummer: an ancient town tracing back to 350 B.C. When Sha-e was established and was officially renamed Riversummer in A.D. 589, one of the three towns that constitutes Wuhan, which now called Chianghsia District under Wuhan.
* Yellow Crane Tower: a famous tower in present-day Wuhan, Hupei Province.
* A phoenix, I've no food with me: The food here refers to pearly stone; a phoenix eats pearly stone and bamboo shoots according to Chinese mythology.

送郄昂谪巴中

瑶草寒不死，
移植沧江滨。
东风洒雨露，
会入天地春。
予若洞庭叶，
随波送逐臣。
思归未可得，
书此谢情人。

Seeing Off Ang Ch'ieh Demoted to Pa

Jade grass, tho it is cold, dies ne'er;
It may transplant to the Blue there.
When East Wind sprinkles it with dew,
It'll grow twixt sky and earth anew.
A fallen leaf on Cavehall blue,
I'll chase a wave to follow you.
I can't go back, my town I miss;
For you, my friend, I now write this.

* the Blue: the Blue River, an unidentified river in this poem.
* Cavehall: a large lake in today's Hunan Province.

江夏送张丞

欲别心不忍，
临行情更亲。
酒倾无限月，
客醉几重春。
藉草依流水，
攀花赠远人。
送君从此去，
回首泣迷津。

Seeing Off Deputy Chang at Riversummer

You will depart, which I do hate;
The farther, the closer, my mate.
The wine is spilled to the moon sunk;
When can I wake up if I'm drunk?
It seems the grass with water flows;
I'd pluck a bloom for him who goes.
Bye, bye, I see you off hereby;
Faced with the hazy ford, I cry.

* Riversummer: an ancient town tracing back to 350 B.C. when Sha-e was established and was officially renamed Riversummer in A.D. 589, one of the three towns that constitutes Wuhan, now called Chianghsia District under Wuhan.
* the moon: the celestial body that revolves around the earth from west to east, which appears at night and gives off shining silvery light, an image of purity and solitude in Chinese culture.
* I'd pluck a bloom for him who goes: A willow twig or a bloom is plucked as a token of farewell, especially in the T'ang dynasty, as often appears in poems.

赋得白鹭鸶送宋少府入三峡

白鹭拳一足，
月明秋水寒。
人惊远飞去，
直向使君滩。

Following the Rhyme of Egrets Seeing Off Sung, the Royal Logistics Manager, to Three Gorges

The egret stands on one foot, still;
The moon does autumn water chill.
Surprised, it spreads its wings to cry;
Right to Prefect Bay, it does fly.

* Three Gorges: referring to the three gorges of the Long River, including Big Pond Gorge, Witch Gorge, and Westridge Gorge.
* egret: a heron characterized, in the breeding season, by long and loose plumes drooping over the tail, usually white plumage.
* the moon: the planet of the earth, which appears at night and gives off shining silvery light, an image of purity and solitude in Chinese culture.
* Prefect Bay: 55 kilometers from Eeridge of today's Eech'ang, Hupei Province.

送二季之江东

初发强中作，
题诗与惠连。
多惭一日长，
不及二龙贤。
西塞当中路，
南风欲进船。
云峰出远海，
帆影挂清川。
禹穴藏书地，
匡山种杏田。
此行俱有适，
迟尔早归旋。

Seeing Off My Two Cousins to East Land

In Stronghold where we will soon part,
I write this verse out of my heart.
It's too short though it's a long day
For my two good cousins to stay.
Through Western Pass you will now go
While south wind to your boat does blow.
Afar, peaks out of clouds appear;
The shades of sails blend with waves clear.
In Worm's Cave, Wordist books you keep;
On Mt. Square apricots you reap.
For this trip there you properly stay,

> Your journey back please don't delay.

* East Land: the east area of the Long River starting from Nine Rivers (Chiuchiang), Chianghsi Province, including part of today's Anhui Province and part of Chiangsu Province.
* Worm's Cave: referring to where Worm, the founding lord of Hsia, was buried.
* Wordist: relating to or derived from Wordism, which is naturalism in most cases. In the T'ang dynasty, an age of proselytism, while Confucianism remained the guiding principle of state and social morality, Wordism had gathered an incrustation of mythology and superstition and was fast winning a following of both the court and the common people. Laocius, the founder, was claimed by the reigning dynasty as its remote progenitor and was honored with an imperial title, Emperor Dark One.
* Mt. Square: about 25 kilometers from Green Lotus, Pai Li's hometown, and Pai Li studied and practiced swordplay for ten years in the Mt. Square Academy here.
* apricot: a tree or the fruit of the tree of the rose family, intermediate between the peach and the plum. Growing, reaping or selling apricots alludes to a hermit who is kind to the folks, just like Feng Tung, who gave free medical treatment to them except that he asked them to plant one to five apricot trees for him according to the severity of their illness.

江西送友人之罗浮

桂水分五岭，
衡山朝九疑。
乡关渺安西，
流浪将何之？
素色愁明湖，
秋渚晦寒姿。
畴昔紫芳意，
已过黄发期。
君王纵疏散，
云壑借巢夷。
尔去之罗浮，
我还憩峨眉。
中阔道万里，
霞月遥相思。
如寻楚狂子，
琼树有芳枝。

Seeing Off My Friend to Mt. La Phu

The Five Ridges see the Cassia flow;
The Nine Doubts face Mt. Scale below.
Pacified West's far from your town;
Where will you rove, like thistledown?
Lake Bright shimmers with a sad touch;
The Shoal's chilled by autumn as such.
The burgeoning twigs as before

Have dried, not in prime any more.
No kings or emperors will long stay,
But hermits can enjoy their day.
You're going to Mt. La Phu now;
I will still rest atop Mt. Brow.
Thousands of miles we're kept apart;
The clouds and moon express our heart.
Like Madman from Ch'u we've no care
The jade tree sways its sprays so fair.

* La Phu: an attractive mountain in today's Kuangtung Province, where Surge Ko, a hermit in the Chin dynasty, used to live in seclusion.
* the Five Ridges: the five hills south of Mt. Scale, rolling east to the sea.
* the Cassia: or the Kui if transliterated, a river that originates from Hunan Province and flows to Cassiawood (Kuilin), implying Cassiawood (Kuilin), a picturesque city in present-day Kuanghsi Province.
* the Nine Doubts: the mountain where Hibiscus was buried, located in Hunan Province. It was so named because it confused people by similar peaks and landscape.
* Mt. Scale: one of the Five Mountains in China, located in Hunan Province, along with Mt. Ever in Shanhsi, Mt. Arch in Shantung, Mt. Flora in Sha'anhsi, and Mt. Tower in Honan.
* Pacified West: referring to Anhsi if transliterated, a protectorate instituted in the T'ang dynasty, located in today's New Land (Hsinchiang).
* But hermits can enjoy their day: an allusion to Nestle and Freedom, who were both hermits of talent and declined to be king when Mound intended to abdicate the throne to them, hence enjoying their casual but happy in the countryside.
* Mt. Brow: one of the four Buddhist mountains, located in Ssuch'uan Province, named for its elegant brow-shaped silhouette viewed from a distance.
* Madman from Ch'u: referring to Tung Lu, a hermit of Ch'u in the Spring and Autumn period, who sang with contempt in front of Confucius, and refused to seek an official career like him. It is said that Lu and his wife lived in seclusion in Mt. Brow and became immortals.

宣州谢朓楼饯别校书叔云

弃我去者，昨日之日不可留；
乱我心者，今日之日多烦忧。
长风万里送秋雁，
对此可以酣高楼。
蓬莱文章建安骨，
中间小谢又清发。
俱怀逸兴壮思飞，
欲上青天览明月。
抽刀断水水更流，
举杯消愁愁更愁。
人生在世不称意，
明朝散发弄扁舟。

Seeing Off Yün, My Uncle, a Collator, on T'iao Hsieh's Tower in Hsuan

What deserts me is yesterday that has gone away;
What disturbs me is today that does me dismay.
The wind blows a thousand miles for wild geese;
Let's go upstairs, let's drink to the spry breeze.
Your verses are pithy with colors clean;
My poems are pretty like branches green.
Full of pride, so elegant, we would fly
To pick up the shining moon from the sky.
Cut off the flow, and we will see more flow;
Drink off our woe, and we will have more woe.

Life is hard, such a harassing affair;
Let's row tomorrow, disheveled our hair.

* T'iao Hsieh: T'iao Hsieh (A.D. 464 - A.D. 499), an outstanding highborn landscape poet. He was appointed prefect of Hsuan in A.D. 495 and then director of the Board of Civil Affairs, and died in prison due to a false charge.
* Hsuan: an ancient town or prefecture in present-day Hsuan, Anhui Province.
* wild goose: an undomesticated goose that is caring and responsible, taken as a symbol of benevolence, righteousness, good manner, wisdom and faith in Chinese culture.
* Your verses are pithy with colors clean: referring to the style of Making Peace, i.e., the third reign title of Emperor Hsien (A.D. 181 - A.D. 234) of Eastern Han, when literature flourished.

宣城送刘副使入秦

君即刘越石，
雄豪冠当时。
凄清横吹曲，
慷慨扶风词。
虎啸俟腾跃，
鸡鸣遭乱离。
千金市骏马，
万里逐王师。
结交楼烦将，
侍从羽林儿。
统兵捍吴越，
豺虎不敢窥。
大勋竟莫叙，
已过秋风吹。
秉钺有季公，
凛然负英姿。
寄深且戎幕，
望重必台司。
感激一然诺，
纵横两无疑。
伏奏归北阙，
鸣驺忽西驰。
列将咸出祖，
英僚惜分离。
斗酒满四筵，
歌啸宛溪湄。
君携东山妓，

我咏北门诗。
贵贱交不易,
恐伤中园葵。
昔赠紫骝驹,
今倾白玉卮。
同欢万斛酒,
未足解相思。
此别又千里,
秦吴渺天涯。
月明关山苦,
水剧陇头悲。
借问几时还,
春风入黄池。
无令长相忆,
折断绿杨枝。

Seeing Off Vice Governor Liu to Ch'in at Hsuan

You are like Kun Liu, called Yüeh Stone,
A pride of prides, the first, well known.
The flute you play, alone and cold;
The air you sing, so loud and bold.
The tiger howls, to leap ahead;
The rooster cries, expelled with dread.
For all gold a fine horse you buy;
The elite troops you follow nigh.
You get along with generals best;
And serve the garrison, the crest.
You safeguard Wu and Yüeh so fast;

E'en tigers there dare not go past.
Your merit great no prize has won;
Blown by west wind, totally gone.
Commander Chi does well command;
How handsomely he waves the wand.
I hope you will hold fast your mace;
One day you'll rule with the Lord's grace.
Thank you for the promise you keep;
The battle field you cleanly sweep.
You'll go and report what you've done;
You gallop your horse and west run.
Your soldiers come out to say bye;
Their farewell song is like a sigh.
At feast all are given to wine;
To the river they sing and whine.
You sing with singing girls from east;
I chant *Northern Gate* to the feast.
It's hard as you're high and I'm dirt;
The yard marrow we shouldn't hurt.
A best colt you gave me before;
I'll drink for you and I'll drink more.
Let's drink more to go on the spree;
But drinking can't quench you and me.
Before long, we will part again;
Ch'in and Wu far away remain.
The bitter moon o'er the pass glows;
The harried stream thru Mt. Bulge flows.
May I ask when you'll come back, when?
Spring wind will cheer Yellow Pool then.
Don't let me wait long, don't fret me
Till I break all sprays off the tree.

* Hsuan: an ancient town or prefecture in present-day Hsuan, Anhui Province.
* Kun Liu: Kun Liu (A.D. 271 – A.D. 318), a statesman, musician, litterateur, strategist in the Chin dynasty, whose courtesy name was Yüeh Stone.
* Wu: the State of Wu (12th Century B.C.–473 B.C.), a vassal state in the lower reaches of the Long River. It was one of the most powerful states in the Spring and Autumn period and was finally annexed by the State of Yüeh, its neighboring state.
* Yüeh: the State of Yüeh (2032 B.C.– 222 B.C.), a vassal state in Southeast China through the ages of Hsia, Shang, and Chough.
* Commander Chi: referring to Kuangchen Chi, a commander in the T'ang dynasty.
* *Northern Gate*: a poem in *The Book of Songs*, the first collection of Chinese poems compiled by Confucius in the 7th Century B.C.
* Ch'in: the Ch'in State or the State of Ch'in (905 B.C – 206 B.C.), one of the most powerful vassal states in the Chough dynasty, which developed into the first unified regime of China, i.e. the Ch'in Empire.
* Mt. Bulge: a mountain located in the southeast of present-day Kansu Province, 2,928 meters above sea level and about 240 kilometers long from north to south, the borderline between Sha'anhsi Loess Plateau and West Bulge Loess Plateau, formerly inhabited by the Ch'iang nationality.

泾川送族弟錞

泾川三百里，
若耶羞见之。
锦石照碧山，
两边白鹭鸶。
佳境千万曲，
客行无歇时。
上有琴高水，
下有陵阳祠。
仙人不见我，
明月空相知。
问我何事来？
卢敖结幽期。
蓬山振雄笔，
绣服挥清词。
江湖发秀色，
草木含荣滋。
置酒送惠连，
吾家称白眉。
愧无海峤作，
敢阙河梁诗。
见尔复几朝，
俄然告将离。
中流漾彩鹢，
列岸丛金羁。
叹息苍梧凤，
分栖琼树枝。
清晨各飞去，

飘落天南垂。
望极落日尽,
秋深暝猿悲。
寄情与流水,
但有长相思。

Seeing Off My Cousin Chun at the Ching Stream

The Ching zigzags three hundred miles
And to the shy Joyeh Stream smiles.
Gilt stone ashore dazzles the eye;
White egrets by the stream will fly.
The mirage flows to bend and bend;
The tourists stroll on without end.
From high the Zither does down flow
Onto Ridgeshine Shrine down below.
The immortal does not come out;
The moon is but friend mine devout.
The moon asks: Why are you here, mate?
With Lodge Pride here I have a date.
He waves his brush like a cascade,
Coming out with verse finely made,
Like lakes and creeks giving hues fine,
Like plants and grass lush with a shine.
I set wine for my cousin now,
Who is my family's high brow.
I've no masterpiece, what a shame!
How dare I write a *Bridge* the same?
For several times I have seen you;

Now rashly you bid me adieu.
Painted pleasure boats drift, drift more;
Gold saddles and bits gleam ashore.
Alas, the phoenix once with me
Will perch on another jade tree.
Tomorrow morn, it will off fly
And light beneath the southern sky.
The sun's setting there, I gaze;
The monkeys cry through autumn haze.
I send my message to the flow;
May it send missing mine to you.

* the Ching Stream: a stream in today's Hsuan, Anhui Province.
* the Joyeh Stream: a stream in the south of present-day Shaohsing. As is said, West Maid did her laundry here.
* the Zither: a stream in State Pacifier Prefecture, i.e. today's Hsuan, Anhui Province.
* Ridgeshine Shrine: Lingyang if transliterated, a county located in present-day Anhui Province. According to legends, Sir Glare became immortal half way to Mt. Ridgeshine, so a shrine was built there in the T'ang dynasty.
* Lodge Pride: an alchemist (275 B.C.- 195 B.C.) in the Ch'in dynasty, who looked for immortals and elixirs for Emperor First and fled the emperor due to his tyranny.
* brush: any of various writing brushes or called Chinese brush, widely used for writing or painting, invented or renovated by Tien Meng (259 B.C.- 210 B.C.), a general in the Ch'in dynasty.
* *Bridge*: referring to a poem *To Wu Su* composed by Ridge Li, the famous Han general.
* phoenix: In Chinese myths, phoenixes, auspicious birds, unlike ordinary ones, only perch on parasol trees, and only eat bamboo shoots and pearly stone.

五松山送殷淑

秀色发江左，
风流奈若何？
仲文了不还，
独立扬清波。
载酒五松山，
颓然白云歌。
中天度落月，
万里遥相过。
抚酒惜此月，
流光畏蹉跎。
明日别离去，
连峰郁嵯峨。

Seeing Off Shu Yin at Mt. Five Pines

Left of the bank a complexion fair,
Who can tell your elegance and flair?
Your talented forbear has gone;
You splash waves here, carrying on.
To Mt. Five Pines, you here wine bring,
And, as if drunk, *White Cloud* you sing.
The moon now moving west to veer,
Thousands of miles off, looking here.
This wine I'd offer to the moon,
Lest time is squandered away soon.
Tomorrow you'll be leaving me;

The mountains high continue to be.

* Shu Yin: a Wordist in the T'ang dynasty, Woodman by Wordist name.
* Mt. Five Pines: a mountain located in today's Tungling, Anhui Province, so named because there grew five pines on the very top. According to *Geographical Wonders* compiled in the Southern Sung dynasty, "The mountain boasted old pines, five in one, a pentad, reaching high to the sky with scale-like bark on the trunk."
* *White Cloud*: a song that Mother West sang for King Solemn of Chough at the Jade Pool.
* the moon: the celestial body that revolves around the earth from west to east, which appears at night and gives off shining silvery light, an image of purity and solitude in Chinese culture.

送崔氏昆季之金陵

放歌倚东楼,
行子期晓发。
秋风渡江来,
吹落山上月。
主人出美酒,
灭烛延清光。
二崔向金陵,
安得不尽觞。
水客弄归棹,
云帆卷轻霜。
扁舟敬亭下,
五两先飘扬。
峡石入水花,
碧流日更长。
思君无岁月,
西笑阻河梁。

Seeing Off the K'un's Brothers to Gold Hill

Against East Tower I sing a song;
The traveler's leaving before long.
An autumn breeze wading the stream
Blows the moon downhill with its gleam.
The host comes out with mellow wine
Blows out the lamp and lets in shine.
They two will for Gold Hill depart,

Why not drink to open our heart?
The boatman there does his oar ply,
The sail touched with hoarfrost on high.
By Mt. Chingt'ing the boat now rows;
The weathercock above high flows.
The gorge stone amid eddies stands;
The sunlit blue afar expands.
I'll miss you year in and year out;
Now I sneer west at the dam stout.

* Gold Hill: referring to Nanking, one of the most well-known ancient cities in China, a strategic fort as a gateway to the sea, which has been the capital of Wu, Chin, and many other states or kingdoms, such as the six empires called Six Dynasties and has flourished immensely with increasing trade and travel.
* Mt. Chingt'ing: a mountain with literary attractions, located nearby Hsuan.
* sneer west: sneer towards Long Peace, the capital.

登黄山凌歊台送族弟溧阳尉济充泛舟赴华阴

鸾乃凤之族,
翱翔紫云霓。
文章辉五色,
双在琼树栖。
一朝各飞去,
凤与鸾俱啼。
炎赫五月中,
朱曦烁河堤。
尔从泛舟役,
使我心魂凄。
秦地无碧草,
南云喧鼓鼙。
君王减玉膳,
早起思鸣鸡。
漕引救关辅,
疲人免涂泥。
宰相作霖雨,
农夫得耕犁。
静者伏草间,
群才满金闺。
空手无壮士,
穷居使人低。
送君登黄山,
长啸倚天梯。
小舟若凫雁,
大舟若鲸鲵。

开帆散长风,
舒卷与云齐。
日久牛渚晦,
苍然夕烟迷。
相思定何许?
沓在洛阳西。

Climbing Mt. Yellow to Rising Mound, Boating with My Cousin Chich'ung, Sheriff of Lishine and Seeing Him Off to Flowershade

Blue birds, born of phoenixes fair
Fly midst hued clouds and purple air.
Their plumes outshine five colors bright;
They perch on a jade tree at night.
One day they fly away and part;
They both shriek and cry out their heart.
The fifth moon the sun is fire-like,
Shining so hot, baking the dyke.
The boat you are going to row,
Which will reduce my heart to rue.
The western land has dry become;
To pray for rain, they beat the drum.
The Lord now does reduce his fare
And rise early to show his care.
Reliefs are shipped through the pass
So that the drought won't folks harass.
The premier's asked for a sweet rain,
So farmers plough their fields again.

The diligent work in grass tall;
The talented fill Golden Hall.
No laziness can make a great one;
All poverty will see one ill done.
Mt. Yellow you're going to scale,
And on the Sky Ladder you'll hail.
Small boats are like ducks and wild geese;
Big boats are like whales ploughing seas.
A strong wind the opened sails furls
And high above the white clouds hurls.
Now late, so dim looms Oxen Shoal;
Amid the haze lost is my soul.
Who do I miss and where is he?
West of Loshine there he might be.

* five colors: referring to five major colors: blue, red, white, black and yellow; a metonymy for various colors, like *The Word and the World* says: "Five colors dazzle the eyes, five sounds deafen the ears, five tastes baffle the palate, galloping to hunt drives one crazy, and rare goods reduce one to misconduct."
* Mt. Yellow: located in today's Anhui Province, one of the most famous mountains in China with natural, literary, and cultural attractions, featured with wondrous pines, clouds and hotsprings. It's said that Lord Yellow as an alchemist used to concoct elixirs here.
* Rising Mound: a summer resort built on Mt. Yellow by Emperor Martial of Sung (A.D. 363 – A.D. 422).
* Lishine: a town in present-day Ch'angchow, Chiangsu Province.
* Flowershade: a town at the foot of Mt. Flower, 120 kilometers from Long Peace, a gateway leading to eight provinces, with a history of more than 2,300 years.
* the Sky Ladder: probably a peak of Mt. Yellow.
* Golden Hall: referring to the imperial academy.
* duck: a web-footed, broad-billed water bird of the *Anatinae* family comprising fresh water and wood ducks, the sea and bay ducks, and the mergansers, a symbol of success in passing Grand Test, i.e., the imperial civil examination in ancient China.
* whale: a cetaceous mammal of fish-like form, especially one of the larger pelagic

species, as distinguished from dolphins and porpoises. Whales have the fore limbs developed as broad flattened paddles, hind limbs absent, and a thick layer of fat or blubber immediately beneath the skin. A whale is a symbol of great ambition, fortitude and uniqueness.

* Oxen Shoal: in Tangt'u County in today's Hsuan, Anhui Province.
* Loshine: Loyang if transliterated, the second largest city and secondary capital of the T'ang Empire.

送储邕之武昌

黄鹤西楼月，
长江万里情。
春风三十度，
空忆武昌城。
送尔难为别，
衔杯惜未倾。
湖连张乐地，
山逐泛舟行。
诺为楚人重，
诗传谢朓清。
沧浪吾有曲，
寄入棹歌声。

Seeing Off Yung Ch'u to Mightboom

The moon shines west o'er Yellow Crane;
The Long River, loving, runs down.
Spring wind has come once and again
In vain I have missed Mightboom Town.
It's hard to say good-bye to you;
So restrained, I won't drink the cup.
The lake links Yellow's Pool with blue;
With your boat the hills will catch up.
Their promise Ch'u folks keep for long;
Your verse like Hsieh's all will adore.
I also have a Blue Wave Song,

Let's sing it to the beat of oar.

* the moon: the planet of the earth, which appears at night and gives off shining silvery light, an image of purity and solitude in Chinese culture.
* Yellow Crane: referring to Yellow Crane Tower built in A.D. 223 in the Three Kingdoms period, a famous tower in present-day Wuhan, Hupei Province.
* the Long River: the longest river in China, originating from the T'angkula Mountains on Tibet Plateau, flowing through 11 provincial areas, more than 6,300 kilometers long, the third longest river in the world.
* Mightboom: referring to Wuch'ang if transliterated, an ancient town and present-day Wuch'ang district in Wuhan.
* Yellow's Pool: referring to Lake Cavehall, because Lord Yellow once played *The Pool* at Lake Cavehall. A passage in *Sir Lush* reads like this—Done Northgate asked Yellow Emperor:"When I first heard you play the tune of *The Pool* in the wild of Cavehall, I felt afraid, then relaxed, and at the end I felt puzzled. I was totally lost in my entrancement."
* Hsieh: T'iao Hsieh (A.D. 464 – A.D. 499), an outstanding highborn landscape poet.
* Blue Wave Song: a song of oar called *West Capital* often sung on the Blue River.

古近体诗三十二首
Old-new Rhythmic Poetry, 32 Poems

酬谈少府

一尉居倏忽，
梅生有仙骨。
三事或可羞，
匈奴哂千秋。
壮心屈黄绶，
浪迹寄沧洲。
昨观荆岘作，
如从云汉游。
老夫当暮矣，
跬足惧骅骝。

A Talk with the Sheriff

Soon as a sheriff you resigned；
Immortal bones in you I find.
A premier's post is not a shame，
Sneered at by the Huns all the same.
To this small post you condescend
While I drift on to the world's end.
I read your Mt. Steep yesterday，
As if I toured the Milky Way.
An old chap, I'm in late years now，
How can I catch up with you, how？

* Hun: one of barbaric nomadic Asian peoples who frequently invaded China, a general term referring to all northern or western invaders.

* Mt. Steep: an important fort in history, located in the southwest of Sowshine (Hsiangyang), the River Han to its east. Here it refers to literary works about Mt. Steep.
* the Milky Way: the Silver River in Chinese mythology, a luminous band circling the heavens composed of stars and nebulae; the Galaxy.

酬宇文少府见赠桃竹书筒

桃竹书筒绮绣文,
良工巧妙称绝群。
灵心圆映三江月,
彩质叠成五色云。
中藏宝诀峨眉去,
千里提携长忆君。

Seeing Yüwen, the Royal Logistics Manager, Who Presents Me with the Peach Bamboo Canister

The peach bamboo's carved with verse like brocade;
Though it's human craft, it's divinely made.
The hollow round looks like the moon downstream,
Its texture layered with five hues that gleam.
To Mt. Brow I take it with knacks there confined,
Like on the way, your love I bear in mind.

* peach bamboo: a species of bamboo with hard wood, used as material for arrows, walking sticks and mats.
* five hues: five major colors, that is, blue, red, white, black and yellow; a metonymy for various colors, like *The Word and the World* says: "Five colors dazzle the eyes, five sounds deafen the ears, five tastes baffle the palate, galloping to hunt drives one crazy, and rare goods reduce one to misconduct."
* Mt. Brow: one of the four Buddhist mountains, located in Ssuch'uan Province, named for its elegant brow-shaped silhouette viewed from a distance.

五月东鲁行答汶上君

五月梅始黄，
蚕凋桑柘空。
鲁人重织作，
机杼鸣帘栊。
顾余不及仕，
学剑来山东。
举鞭访前途，
获笑汶上翁。
下愚忽壮士，
未足论穷通。
我以一箭书，
能取聊城功。
终然不受赏，
羞与时人同。
西归去直道，
落日昏阴虹。
此去尔勿言，
甘心为转蓬。

A Reply to the Sneering Man on the Wen River on My Way to East Lu in the Fifth Moon

In the fifth moon plums start to ripe,
For silk, no leaves left, any type.
Lu folks have a loom in each room,
And shuttles tic tac for their boom.

Of officialdom I've no sense;
I come here to learn swordplay hence.
To ask the way I come ahead,
And I'm sneered at by you instead.
All ambitious men I despise;
What matters if I fall or rise?
With my letter on arrow bound,
I can take Liaoton to take ground.
I'll take no title from the court,
To keep away from the vain sort.
I'll go all my way to the west;
E'en the sun is by clouds depressed.
Of this trip nothing you should say;
Like thistledown I'll drift my way.

* plum: a kind of plant or the edible purple drupaceous fruit of the plant which is any one of various trees of the genus *Prunus*, cultivated in temperate zones.
* Liaoton: Liaoch'eng if transliterated. In the Warring States period, the State of Ch'i lost a lot of soldiers when they tried to retake Liaoton. Chunglien Lu, a sophist of Ch'i wrote a letter and launched it into the city. Persuaded by the letter, the commander in Liaoton committed suicide and left the city to Ch'i.
* thistledown: the pappus of a thistle; the ripe silky fibers from the dry flower of a thistle, a metaphor for drifting or wandering.

早秋单父南楼酬窦公衡

白露见日灭，
红颜随霜凋。
别君若俯仰，
春芳辞秋条。
泰山嵯峨夏云在，
疑是白波涨东海。
散为飞雨川上来，
遥帷却卷清浮埃。
知君独坐青轩下，
此时结念同怀者。
我闭南楼看道书，
幽帘清寂在仙居。
曾无好事来相访，
赖尔高文一起予。

To Heng Tou in South Mansion in Shanfu on an Early Autumn Day

When the sun comes out, the dew's dry;
Once frost beaten, all flowers will die.
Since you left, it's brief like a nod;
The bloom has changed into a pod!
Over Mt. Arch aloft summer clouds be,
As if white waves surge on over East Sea.
They're dispersed into rain and downstream hurled,
Hurling up dust onto your curtain pearled.

　　　　I know sitting in your room you must be
　　　　And at the same time keep thinking of me.
　　　　In South Mansion a Wordist book I read;
　　　　It's like where a quiet life immortals lead.
　　　　But there's no one to come to drink a cup;
　　　　Why don't you write a verse to cheer me up?

* Shanfu: an old county called Shan County, in present-day Shantung Province.
* Mt. Arch: one of the five especially sacred mountains in China, one for each of the four directions and one at the center. Mt. Arch, in the east in today's Shantung Province, is the most revered of the five, as its name may suggest, and its summit is the destination of many pilgrims. Mt. Arch complex includes many lower ridges and summits. The other four mountains are Mt. Ever, west in Shanhsi, Mt. Scale, south in Hunan, Mt. Flora, north in Sha'anhsi, and Mt. Tower, the central one in Honan.
* East Sea: what is East China Sea today, with an area of 770 thousand square kilometers.
* But there's no one to come to drink a cup: Man Yang (53 B.C.- A.D. 18), an outstanding rhymed verse writer and official in the Han dynasty, was once poor and addicted to alcohol.
* Wordist: relating to or derived from Wordism, a follower or practitoner of the naturalist Wordist philosophy, which promulgates the doctrine of non-action or quietism.

山 中 问 答

问余何意栖碧山，
笑而不答心自闲。
桃花流水窅然去，
别有天地非人间。

Question and Answer in the Hills

Asked why Mt. Blue I am willing to dwell;
My heart at ease, I smile but will not tell.
The peach blossoms on the ripples flow by;
It's a Fairyland between earth and sky.

* Fairyland: an imaginary ideal place for Wordist immortals, used as a metaphor in this poem.

答友人赠乌纱帽

领得乌纱帽，
全胜白接䍦。
山人不照镜，
稚子道相宜。

In Reply to My Friend's Gift of a Black Gauze Hat

Thank you for your black gauze hat,
Better than a white cap to look at.
A mirror? I've no need for it;
My child says it's a perfect fit.

* black gauze hat: usually a metaphor for an official position, an important sign in a bureaucratic and meritocratic society like ancient China.

酬张司马赠墨

上党碧松烟，
夷陵丹砂末。
兰麝凝珍墨，
精光乃堪掇。
黄头奴子双鸦鬟，
锦囊养之怀袖间。
今日赠余兰亭去，
兴来洒笔会稽山。

To Commander Chang, Who Gives Me Ink

In Shangtang, we have green pine tar;
From Eeridge comes red cinnabar.
The thoroughwort and musk make ink,
Which does give off a shining blink.
It's like my lovely maiden's crow-black hair;
It's like balm in the sac in her sleeve fair.
To Orchid Kiosk with this I'll go today;
On Mt. Summit, join a verse club I may.

* Shangtang: a prefecture in the T'ang dynasty, in today's Ch'angchih, Shanhsi Province.
* Eeridge: a prefecture in the T'ang dynasty, in today's Eech'ang, Hupei Province.
* cinnabar: a crystallized red mercuric sulfide, HgS, the chief ore of mercury, the raw mineral material for elixir in Wordist alchemy.
* thoroughwort: a stout, fragrant hairy herb, the boneset, 2 to 5 feet high, with white

flowers.
* musk: a soft, reddish-brown powdery secretion of a penetrating odor, obtained from the preputial follicles of the male musk deer, used by perfumers and in medicine.
* Orchid Kiosk: the place where the most famous calligrapher Hsichih Wang and other scholars often gathered for literary activities, in present-day Shaohsing, Chechiang Province.
* Mt. Summit: referring to the K'uaichi Mountains in present-day Chechiang Province, where Worm convened a summit attended by vassal lords, hence the name.

答湖州迦叶司马问白是何人

青莲居士谪仙人，
酒肆藏名三十春。
湖州司马何须问，
金粟如来是后身。

In Reply to Commander Kasyapa of Laketon, Who Asks Me Who I Am

An exiled saint, Green Lotus is my name;
For Thirty years in wine I've sunk my fame.
Commander Laketon, you need not ask me;
Gold Millet Buddha is what I would be.

* Green Lotus: Pai Li's Wordist name.
* Laketon: Huchow if transliterated, located in present-day Chechiang Province.
* Gold Millet Buddha: Vimalakīrti, a representative figure in Buddhism.

答长安崔少府叔封游终南翠微寺太宗皇帝金沙泉见寄

河伯见海若,
傲然夸秋水。
小物昧远图,
宁知通方士。
多君紫霄意,
独往苍山里。
地古寒云深,
岩高长风起。
初登翠微岭,
复憩金沙泉。
践苔朝霜滑,
弄波夕月圆。
饮彼石下流,
结萝宿溪烟。
鼎湖梦渌水,
龙驾空茫然。
早行子午关,
却登山路远。
拂琴听霜猿,
灭烛乃星饭。
人烟无明异,
鸟道绝往返。
攀崖倒青天,
下视白日晚。
既过石门隐,
还唱石潭歌。

涉雪搴紫芳,
濯缨想清波。
此人不可见,
此地君自过。
为余谢风泉,
其如幽意何。

In Reply to Shufeng Ts'ui, Sheriff of Long Peace, Who Tours Emperor Grandsire's Sand Spring in Greenhill Temple in the South Mountains

River God did to Sea God boast:
Autumn water's wondrous, the most.
A flunky knows not a great plan;
He only knows a Wordist man.
If one wants to know what things are,
He'd go to the mountains afar.
The earth so cold, cold clouds seem deep;
The crags so high, high wind does sweep.
The green ridge he can at first climb,
And at Sand Spring rest for some time.
Moss frost shines on slippery ground;
Waves are splashed to the moon so round.
He may drink what beneath stone flows,
Where a vine with the creek mist goes.
Lake Tripod ripples in his dream;
A dragon flies through a void beam.
Morn sees him through Meridian Pass;
His far climbing does him harass.

He plays the lute to monkeys' cries
And dines beneath the starlit skies.
No souls at all, all people gone,
The bird track has no more birds on.
Climbing high, he sees the sky below
And the sun setting faintly glow.
Thru Stone Gate with a shady cool,
He still sings the song of Stone Pool.
He picks purple grass from the snow,
And cleans his tassel in the flow.
If this man you don't want to see,
You go your way and let him be.
Thank you for showing me Wind Spring,
What does the shade there to you bring?

* Long Peace: Ch'ang'an if transliterated, the capital of T'ang, with 1,000,000 inhabitants, the largest walled city ever built by man, and a cosmopolis of world religions, Buddhism, Confucianism, Wordism, Nestorianism, Zoroastrianism, and even Islamism represented by Saracens. It was the wonder of the age that reached the pinnacle of brilliance in Emperor Deepsire's reign: The main castle with its nine-fold gates, the thirty-six imperial palaces, pillars of gold, innumerable mansions, towers and villas of noblemen, the broad avenues thronged with motley crowds of townsfolk, gallants on horseback, and mandarin cars drawn by yokes of black oxen, countless taverns and houses of pleasure, which opened their doors by night all made this city a kaleidoscope of miracles.
* River God did to Sea God boast: referring to a dialogue between River God, i.e., God of the Yellow River, and Sea God in *Sir Lush*. At River God's boasting, Sea God replied:"A frog cannot understand the sea talked to it due to its limit of surroundings; a summer insect cannot understand the ice talked to it due to its limit of time; a rustic cannot understand the Word talked to him due to his limit of education. Now you've come from a shoal to see a sea and realized your ugliness, I can talk about great truth with you."
* Emperor Grandsire: Shimin Li (A.D. 598 – A. D. 649), the second emperor of T'ang, an eminent politician, strategist, militarist and poet.

* the South Mountains: one of the mountains of Ch'in Ridge, where dwelt many hermits, located to the south of Long Peace, Sha'anhsi Province. It is also known Mt. Earthlungs, a great stronghold of the capital, towering in the middle of Ch'in Ridge and rolling about 100 kilometers. It is the birthplace of Wordist culture, Buddhist culture, Filial Piety culture, Longevity culture, Bellheads culture and Plutus culture and is praised as the Capital of Fairies, the crown of Heavenly Abode and the Promised Land of the World.
* Wordist: relating to or derived from the doctrines declared by Laocius (571 B.C.-471 B.C.).
* Lake Tripod: the lake where Lord Yellow became immortal and rode a dragon to fly to the sky.
* dragon: Though variously understood as a large reptile, a marine monster, a jackal and so on in Western culture, it has been esteemed as a fabulous serpent-like giant winged animal, a totem of the Chinese nation and a symbol of benevolence and sovereignty in Chinese culture.
* Meridian Pass: an important passage from Long Peace, the capital, to Mid-Han, Pa, Shu and other southern areas.

酬崔五郎中

朔云横高天,
万里起秋色。
壮士心飞扬,
落日空叹息。
长啸出原野,
凛然寒风生。
幸遭圣明时,
功业犹未成。
奈何怀良图,
郁悒独愁坐。
杖策寻英豪,
立谈乃知我。
崔公生民秀,
缅邈青云姿。
制作参造化,
托讽含神祇,
海岳尚可倾,
吐诺终不移。
是时霜飙寒,
逸兴临华池。
起舞拂长剑,
四座皆扬眉。
因得穷欢情,
赠我以新诗。
又结汗漫期,
九垓远相待。
举身憩蓬壶,

濯足弄沧海。
从此凌倒景，
一去无时还。
朝游明光宫，
暮入闾阖关。
但得长把袂，
何必嵩丘山。

To Ts'ui Five, the Royal Guard

Northern clouds hang in the high skies;
The vast land sees autumn hues rise.
With a great aim, you're a great one;
Now you sigh to the setting sun.
The wild resounds with your long wow,
Which with force stirs up a chill sough.
Blessed to have been born at good time,
Unfulfilled, a height you need climb.
Although a blueprint in your chest,
You sit there alone, so depressed.
With your stick a hero you'd find;
Just a brief talk, you know my mind.
Dear Ts'ui, you've the great altitude,
So detached with your solitude.
Made by Nature, there you'd abide;
Gods and goddesses you deride.
The mountains may fall, low or steep;
Your promise, once made, you fast keep.
A cold sough blows o'er frosty cool;
Inspired, you come near to Clear Pool.

You play your sword and so you dance;
The audience's mood you enhance.
Having been applauded with glee,
You compose a new verse for me.
Now, you'll travel afar and high
And be received out of the sky.
In Fairyland you'll take a seat
And in Blue Sea you'll wash your feet.
From here you see scenes upside down,
And will ne'er come back to your town.
At dawn you tour Light Palace great;
At dusk you enter Heaven's Gate.
If you wave your sleeve heart and soul,
Why care about the Towering Knoll?

* Clear Pool: a name that can be found in *Ch'u Lyrics*.
* Fairyland: an imaginary ideal place for Wordist immortals.
* Blue Sea: referring to the changing world in general.
* Light Palace: an imperial palace in the Han dynasty, implying the palaces in Loshine.
* Heaven's Gate: a name shared by many mountains. The one here may indicate a mountain that immortals dwell.
* the Towering Knoll: referring to Mt. Tower, one of the Five Mountains in China, located in Honan Province, along with Mt. Ever in Shanhsi, Mt. Arch in Shantung, Mt. Flora in Sha'anhsi, and Mt. Scale in Hunan.

以诗代书答元丹丘

青鸟海上来，
今朝发何处？
口衔云锦书，
与我忽飞去。
鸟去凌紫烟，
书留绮窗前。
开缄方一笑，
乃是故人传。
故人深相勖，
忆我劳心曲。
离居在咸阳，
三见秦草绿。
置书双袂间，
引领不暂闲。
长望杳难见，
浮云横远山。

In Reply to Redknoll Yüan with a Verse Instead of a Letter

The bluebird comes here from the sea;
Today where will it fly to be?
It brings me a silk letter here;
And does suddenly disappear.
The letter is left by the door;
The bird does o'er purple clouds soar.

I open the envelope and grin;

My old friend's message is within.

He cares about me with concern;

Now ill, to see me he does yearn.

He lives in Allshine, on me keen;

Three times he's seen grass turning green.

I place the letter in my sleeve

And gaze at the skyline and grieve.

He's nowhere and I look around;

Clouds hang over the distant mound.

* Redknoll Yüan: a Wordist and an important friend of Pai Li's. Pai Li met him at the age of twenty and once lived in seclusion with him on Mt. Tower. With their twenty-four years' friendship and correspondence, Rendknoll exerted great influence on Pai Li, who wrote 14 poems dedicated to the former.
* the bluebird: The ancients regarded the bluebird as a courier of immortals.
* silk letter: a term of respect for other's letter or message.
* Allshine: the ancient capital of Ch'in, present-day Hsienyang, Sha'anhsi Province. It was so called because all its rivers and mountains could get sunshine from all around. It was built in 350 B.C. and Ch'in moved its capital here the next year from Oakshine (Liyang).

金门答苏秀才

君还石门日,
朱火始改木。
春草如有情,
山中尚含绿。
折芳愧遥忆,
永路当自勖。
远见故人心,
平生以此足。
巨海纳百川,
麟阁多才贤。
献书入金阙,
酌醴奉琼筵。
屡忝白云唱,
恭闻黄竹篇。
恩光照拙薄,
云汉希腾迁。
铭鼎倘云遂,
扁舟方渺然。
我留在金门,
君去卧丹壑。
未果三山期,
遥欣一丘乐。
玄珠寄象罔,
赤水非寥廓。
愿狎东海鸥,
共营西山药。
栖岩君寂灭,

处世余龙蠖。
良辰不同赏,
永日应闲居。
鸟吟檐间树,
花落窗下书。
缘溪见绿篠,
隔岫窥红蕖。
采薇行笑歌,
眷我情何已。
月出石镜间,
松鸣风琴里。
得心自虚妙,
外物空颓靡。
身世如两忘,
从君老烟水。

In Reply to Su, a Showcharm at Gold Gate

When you to Stone Gate did return,
Firestone was changed to wood to burn.
If spring grass has feeling so keen,
The mountains there should be still green.
Breaking a twig, I think of you,
We'd boost each other while we go.
I know your heart though you're afar;
Be content with this as we are.
The great sea does welcome all streams;
Unicorn Hall with talents teems.
I proffer my verse to Gold Hall
And at feast I toast to peers, to all.

A song of *White Clouds* in the Blue;
And a verse of Yellow Bamboo.
A low one, I've Lord's graceful ray;
I may rise to the Milky Way.
I wish to carve my name with pride
And then canoe to chase a tide.
In Gold Gate here I might just stay;
Lie in Cinnabar Trench you may.
Three Mountains I've no chance to climb;
Beside the knoll, you've a good time.
The lost black pearl No Icon regained;
The Red River narrow remained.
With seagulls at East Sea I'd play;
Or for Western Hill pills we'll stay.
Upon the rock you'll be raised;
Like inchworms I may be debased.
Though the happy hour we can't share,
Let's be free all day, free of care.
Between eaves and trees warblers call;
To my window-side book flowers fall.
You see green bamboo by the rill;
I have red lilies near the hill.
I pick vetch and I sing with glee;
Be free, don't worry about me.
The moon to the Stone Mirror shines;
The Organ blows to the old pines.
With heart, you feel a subtle void;
The world makes one old, all destroyed.
If I could forget all twofold,
I'd follow you through mist till old.

* showcharm: a talent recommended for official use through civil-service examinations or a well-learned person in ancient China, very well respected in a meritocratic and bureaucratic society like China.
* breaking a twig: an allusion to *Breaking Willow*, an ancient tune listed among twenty-four airs for the flute by Conservatoire of Han. Breaking off withies from a willow on the riverbank by a certain bridge outside Long Peace has been used as a symbol of reluctant parting.
* Unicorn Hall: built by Ho Hsiao early in the Han dynasty in Non-end Palace for the storage of books and memory of talented scholars and meritorious generals. The Hall was so named in memory of the event that Emperor Martial once caught a unicorn.
* Gold Hall: referring to the Lord's dwelling.
* *White Clouds*: referring to the song that Mother West sang for King Solemn of Chough at Jade Pool.
* Yellow Bamboo: referring to the verse that King Solemn of Chough wrote for the people who died in a snow storm.
* the Milky Way: the Silver River in Chinese mythology, a luminous band circling the heavens composed of stars and nebulae; the Galaxy.
* Cinnabar Trench: an imaginary place where alchemists refine cinnabar for elixir.
* Three Mountains: referring to the three fairy isles on East Sea.
* The lost black pearl No Icon regained: No Icon regained the pearl Lord Yellow lost. *Sir Lush* reads like this: Then he (Lord Yellow) asked Non Icon to look for it, and he found it. Yellow Emperor exclaimed: "Strange! Why could Non Icon find it?"
* the Red River: a river in Kuichow Province.
* seagull: a kind of sea bird, any gull or large tern, a symbol of clean integrity. The seagulls in the Wordist book *Sir Line* (Liehtzu) are particularly sensitive to impurity of motive and will make friends only with the completely guileless and disinterested.
* East Sea: East China Sea, with an area of 770 thousand square kilometers.
* Western Hill: where two fairies made elixir pills.
* the Stone Mirror: probably a place in the mountains where Showcharm Su is going.
* the Organ: probably a place in the mountains where Showcharm Su is going.

酬坊州王司马与阎正字对雪见赠

游子东南来，
自宛适京国。
飘然无心云，
倏忽复西北。
访戴昔未偶，
寻嵇此相得。
愁颜发新欢，
终宴叙前识。
阎公汉庭旧，
沈郁富才力。
价重铜龙楼，
声高重门侧。
宁期此相遇，
华馆陪游息。
积雪明远峰，
塞城锁春色。
主人苍生望，
假我青云翼。
风水如见资，
投竿佐皇极。

In Reply to Commander Wang of Fangchow and Collator Yan, Facing Snow

A vagrant, I've, from Southeast Land
Called Wen, come to Capital grand.

Much like a cloud without a heart,
All too soon for Northwest I start.
Then I failed to find Tai, my mate;
Now I have met you two, so great.
My saddened face is now lit up;
Let us at this feast drink our cup.
Mister Yan, you have served the court,
Full of vigor, a sunny sport.
Your price outweighs Bronze Dragon's weight;
Your fame's higher than the palace gate.
This encounter I cherish best;
I'd escort you to tour and rest.
The distant hills capped with thick snow,
The frontier town locked in spring hue.
Our Lord loves all creatures on earth;
May He give me wings to fly forth.
Good wind or water is much gold;
The great splendor I would uphold.

* Wen: a fief called Wen in the Warring States period, Wen County in Ch'in's age and Southshine in the Sui and T'ang dynasties, today's Southshine (Nanyang), Honan Province.
* Capital: referring to Long Peace, the capital of T'ang, a cosmopolis with a population of about one million at that time, the largest walled city ever built by man, the center of world religions, Buddhism, Confucianism, Wordism, Nestorianism, Zoroastrianism, and even Islamism represented by Saracens, and the center of education—There were colleges of various grades and special institutes for calligraphy, arithmetic, music, astronomy and so on.
* Bronze Dragon: a bronze dragon statue. There is a bronze dragon on Dragon Gate Tower according to *Han's Book*.

酬中都小吏携斗酒双鱼于逆旅见赠

鲁酒若琥珀,
汶鱼紫锦鳞。
山东豪吏有俊气,
手携此物赠远人。
意气相倾两相顾,
斗酒双鱼表情素。
双鳃呀呷鳍鬣张,
拨剌银盘欲飞去。
呼儿拂几霜刃挥,
红肌花落白雪霏。
为君下箸一餐饱,
醉著金鞍上马归。

To the Clerk from Mid-town, Who Gives Me Wine and Two Fish in an Inn

The Lu wine, amber-like, does shine;
The Wen fish have scales, brocade fine.
The gallant clerk is handsome, with great zest;
He gives the two presents to me, his guest.
He loves me so and I love him no less;
With wine and two fish, we ourselves express.
Its two gills puff, its fins spread, it does splash,
And out of the silver plate it will dash.
A child I call to take a knife so bright;
The red flesh is like blossoms in snow white.

Chopsticks urged, we've had a fabulous meal;
You get on your saddle, and drunk I feel.

* Mid-town: name of a prefecture in Lu, today's Shantung Province.
* Lu: referring to present-day Shantung Province, the State of Lu in the Spring and Autumn period.
* the Wen: the Wen River, 12 kilometers north of Mid-town in today's Honan Province.

酬张卿夜宿南陵见赠

月出鲁城东，
明如天上雪。
鲁女惊莎鸡，
鸣机应秋节。
当君相思夜，
火落金风高。
河汉挂户牖，
欲济无轻舠。
我昔辞林丘，
云龙忽相见。
客星动太微，
朝去洛阳殿。
尔来得茂彦，
七叶仕汉馀。
身为下邳客，
家有圯桥书。
傅说未梦时，
终当起岩野。
万古骑辰星，
光辉照天下。
与君各未遇，
长策委蒿莱。
宝刀隐玉匣，
锈涩空莓苔。
遂令世上愚，
轻我土与灰。
一朝攀龙去，

蛙黾安在哉？
故山定有酒，
与之倾金罍。

In Reply to Shuming Chang Putting Up for the Night at Southridge

The moon east of Luton does glow,
As bright as the Heavenly snow.
Taking the katydid aback,
The Lu maid works her loom, tic-tac.
You may miss someone at night now;
Fire gone, there blows an autumn sough.
In the Milky Way looms a door;
I'd go, but I've no boat or oar.
Then I leave the mountain and grove
While clouds meet a dragon above.
A meteor shoots beside the grand star;
I leave at dawn for Loshine afar.
There have been talents in the land;
The Seven have served Han lords' wand.
Like the one from Hsiap'i you look;
At home you study the war book.
Fu in your dream is not around;
At last he is by a crag found.
As e'er, he rides the morning star,
Lighting up the world near and far.
Now, you are unrequited, man;
In the wormwood you make your plan.
Hide our swords in a cask we must,

E'en if with mould and moss they rust.
All people are foolish, not wise;
Our talent as dirt they despise.
One day a dragon we can ride;
Where will the frogs be, left aside?
There must be wine on the old hill;
Let's take gold cups and drink our fill.

* the moon: the celestial body that revolves around the earth from west to east, which appears at night and gives off shining silvery light, an image of purity and solitude in Chinese culture.
* Luton: the capital of Lu, present-day Chockfull (Ch'üfu), Shantung Province.
* katydid: any of several large, green orthopteran insects, having long lender antennae and long hind legs: the male has highly developed stridulating organs on the forewings, that produce a shrill sound.
* the Milky Way: a luminous band circling the heavens composed of stars and nebulae; the Galaxy.
* dragon: a fabulous serpent-like giant winged animal that can change its girth and length, a symbol of benevolence and sovereignty in Chinese culture.
* Loshine: Loyang if transliterated, the second largest city in the T'ang dynasty, when it had about 800,000 inhabitants.
* the one from Hsiap'i: referring to Liang Chang (? - 186 B.C.), a prominent statesman and counsellor, and one of the founders of Han. In Hsiap'i, he met Yellow Stone, a legendary Wordist, and got *The Art of War*.
* Hsiap'i: a place tracing back to the Warring State period, a fief, then he capital of a prefecture early in the Han dynasty, a vassal state enfeoffed to Hsin Han in 202 B.C. and a kingdom in the Emperor Bright of Han period, a place of strategic importance.
* Fu: referring to Yüeh Fu (Master Joy), an official of virtue in the Shang dynasty. Historic records say that the King of Shang dreamed of a sage, and he sent people out to search for the sage and found Yüeh Fu.
* frog: one of a genus of (*Rana*) of small, tailless, amphibious, web-footed animal, usually alluding to good harvest or prosperity in Chinese culture.

酬岑勋见寻就元丹丘对酒相待以诗见招

黄鹤东南来，
寄书写心曲。
倚松开其缄，
忆我肠断续。
不以千里遥，
命驾来相招。
中逢元丹丘，
登岭宴碧霄。
对酒忽思我，
长啸临清飙。
蹇予未相知，
茫茫绿云垂。
俄然素书及，
解此长渴饥。
策马望山月，
途穷造阶墀。
喜兹一会面，
若睹琼树枝。
忆君我远来，
我欢方速至。
开颜酌美酒，
乐极忽成醉。
我情既不浅，
君意方亦深。
相知两相得，
一顾轻千金。

且向山客笑，
与君论素心。

To Hsun Tsen, Who Calls on Me, Talking About Redknoll Yüan's Treating Him with Wine and Verse

The yellow crane from southeast comes,
Sending me a song his heart hums.
I ope the letter 'gainst the pine,
Recalling how my soul did whine.
To see you I'd drive all the way;
Three hundred miles was nothing, nay.
I met Redknoll Yüan half way there;
Uphill we drank in the green air.
For all missing, drinking is enow;
we uttered a howl to the sough.
Wow, friend, if I had not you known,
The green cloud would hang there alone.
To write you a letter I burst
So as to quench my long time thirst.
I spur my horse, gaze at the moon
And build steps for you to come soon.
O I meet you there, what a glee,
As if I've seen the jadeite tree.
You thought I would come from afar;
Now I'm here, how happy we are!
We drink wine, we laugh and we smile,
And we get drunk in a short while.
Not shallow is my emotion

And yours is deep like an ocean.
If each other we know and hold,
We can throw away all that gold.
To the mountain hermit let's smile;
We'll talk heart to heart, free of guile.

* Redknoll Yüan: a Wordist and an important friend of Pai Li's. Pai met him at the age of twenty and once lived in seclusion with him on Mt. Tower. With their twenty-four years' friendship and correspondence, Rendknoll exerted great influence on Pai Li, who wrote 14 poems dedicated to the former.

答从弟幼成过西园见赠

一身自潇洒，
万物何嚣喧。
拙薄谢明时，
栖闲归故园。
二季过旧壑，
四邻驰华轩。
衣剑照松宇，
宾徒光石门。
山童荐珍果，
野老开芳樽。
上陈樵渔事，
下叙农圃言。
昨来荷花满，
今见兰苕繁。
一笑复一歌，
不知夕景昏。
醉罢同所乐，
此情难具论。

In Reply to Yuch'eng, My Cousin, Who Calls on Me in West Garden

You are so free, with grace and ease;
How noisy, how vain the world is!
At this good time I'm rough and low,
So back to the farmland I'll go.

My cousin comes to where I dwell;
My neighbors come in carts as well.
Their swords and robes shine, so ornate
E'en their suite glows to the stone gate.
Kids proffer their fruits, the whole lot;
Old men open their hoarded pot.
We talk how we fish and cut wood;
They tell how they grow crops for food.
Yesterday lotus blooms did teem;
Today blooms of trumpet vine beam.
We laugh and then we sing a song,
Not knowing night comes along.
Do drink more and join in the glee;
What I want to say does fail me.

* lotus: one of the various plants of the waterlily family, noted for their large floating leaves and showy flowers, an important image in Chinese culture; in most cases it is associated with Buddhism, for example, Pai Li has various names, one of which is Green Lotus Buddhist.
* trumpet: a pitcher plant with slender, erect, hollow leaves and long creepers.

酬王补阙惠翼庄庙宋丞泚赠别

学道三千春，
自言羲和人。
轩盖宛若梦，
云松长相亲。
偶将二公合，
复与三山邻。
喜结海上契，
自为天外宾。
鸾翻我先铩，
龙性君莫驯。
朴散不尚古，
时讹皆失真。
勿踏荒溪坂，
揭来浩然津。
薜带何辞楚，
桃源堪避秦。
世迫且离别，
心在期隐沦。
酬赠非炯诫，
永言铭佩绅。

Thanks to E Wang, the Remonstrant, and Tz'u Sung, the Manager of Huichuang Temple, Who Write Me Poems of Farewell

The Word learned for three thousand years,

She-her and I have become peers!
The canopy looms like a dream;
Clouds and pines are close, so I deem.
As soon as the two are combined,
They are with Three Mountains aligned.
With those from the sea I will stay
And join those in the Milky Way.
Blue birds' plumage I will first break;
Dragons sleeping you should not wake.
Not simple, as they used to do,
A mistake, they've lost what is true.
Don't tread on the wild riv'rine slope;
Come to Broad Ford, a ford of hope.
With fiscus belt, in Ch'u you'd be;
To Peach Source from Ch'in you flee.
From the troubled world go apart;
Mountains and rivers please your heart.
My gift may not be best advice;
It can be worn as a badge nice.

* the Word: referring to Tao if transliterated, the most significant and profoundest concept in Chinese philosophy. According to Laocius's *The Word and the World*: "The Word is void, but its use is infinite. O deep! It seems to be the root of all things."
* She-her: the mother of the sun or the dyad of Goddess of Sun and Goddess of Calendar in Chinese mythology.
* Three Mountains: referring to the three fairy isles on East Sea.
* the Milky Way: known as the Silver River in Chinese culture, a luminous band circling the heavens composed of stars and nebulae; the Galaxy.
* dragon: a fabulous serpent-like giant winged animal, a symbol of benevolence and sovereignty in Chinese culture.
* fiscus belt: an image in Chü Yüan's poem.
* Ch'u: a vassal state of Chough, one of the powers in the Warring States period, conquered and annexed by Ch'in in 223 B.C.

* Peach Source: Peach Blossom Source. According to Yüanming Tao's writing, a group of Ch'in people fled to Peach Blossom Source to keep away from the turbulent days, and the people and their offsprings had lived an idyllic and isolated life for 500 years before a fisherman of Chin stumbled into the village.
* Ch'in: the Ch'in State or the State of Ch'in (905 B.C.- 206 B.C.), one of the most powerful vassal states in the Chough dynasty, which developed into the first unified regime of China, i.e. the Ch'in Empire.

酬裴侍御对雨感时见赠

雨色秋来寒,
风严清江爽。
孤高绣衣人,
潇洒青霞赏。
平生多感激,
忠义非外奖。
祸连积怨生,
事及徂川往。
楚邦有壮士,
鄢郢翻扫荡。
申包哭秦庭,
泣血将安仰。
鞭尸辱已及,
堂上罗宿莽。
颇似今之人,
蟊贼陷忠谠。
渺然一水隔,
何由税归鞅。
日夕听猿怨,
怀贤盈梦想。

In Reply to P'ei, the Royal Servant, Who Dedicates a Poem to Me While Viewing a Rain

An autumn rain makes it cold now;

Across the river blows a sough.
You're solitary in brocade,
An immortal, divinely made.
In life you have done well and much,
Loyal and righteous, praised as such.
Upheavals and chaos rush on;
All merits and credits have gone.
In Ch'u there rose a man so brave,
Who swept Yan-Ying like a huge wave.
Fleeing to Ch'in's court, Shen there cried
Till he bled and to the sky sighed.
The corpse whipping was such a shame
That halls and tombs lay waste, the same.
Lo, all those who wield power today
With cheats and thieves the worthies slay.
Now by that river kept apart,
How can I go back in my cart?
Day and night I hear monkeys scream,
And meet you only in my dream.

* In Ch'u there rose a man so brave: referring to Tsehsu Wu (559 B.C.- 484 B.C.), a renowned minister of Wu. In 522 B.C., Tsehsu Wu escaped from Ch'u when his father and elder brother had been killed by King Peace. After nine years' preparation, he led an army to wipe out Ch'u. By then, King Peace had been dead, so Wu dug out his corpse and whipped it for revenge.
* Yan-Ying: referring to the capital of Ch'u.
* Shen: referring to Paohsu Shen, a senior official of Ch'u in the Spring and Autumn period. In order to revive his motherland, Shen went to Ch'in and cried for seven days to ask for help which moved the lord and officials in Ch'in.

酬崔侍御

严陵不从万乘游,
归卧空山钓碧流。
自是客星辞帝座,
元非太白醉扬州。

In Reply to Ts'ui, the Royal Servant

Yan wouldn't serve the Lord as all would do;
He went back to hills and fished by the blue.
A meteor, I bid farewell to the throne;
I'm not Venus that lies drunk and alone.

* Yan: referring to Tsuling Yan (39 B.C.– A.D. 41), a renowned hermit in the Han dynasty. He showed his talent at an early age. After Hsiu Liu was enthroned to be the emperor of Han, Yan was invited several times to serve the court. Though the emperor was an acquaintance of his, Yan declined the offer and chose to live in seclusion in the Richspring Hills.
* Venus: Pai Li's given name, which is what pai denotes in Chinese. On the night of the poet's birth his mother dreamed of the planet of Venus, which is the Morning Star in the morning and the Evening Star in the evening, as *The Book of Songs* says: "Here shines east Morning Star; Here veers west Evening Star". Our poet was given the name Venus, literally Pai or T'aipai, which suggests he was a descendant of the spirit of Venus.

玩月金陵城西孙楚酒楼,达曙歌吹,日晚乘醉著紫绮裘乌纱巾,与酒客数人棹歌秦淮,往石头访崔四侍御

昨玩西城月,
青天垂玉钩。
朝沽金陵酒,
歌吹孙楚楼。
忽忆绣衣人,
乘船往石头。
草裹乌纱巾,
倒被紫绮裘。
两岸拍手笑,
疑是王子猷。
酒客十数公,
崩腾醉中流。
谑浪棹海客,
喧呼傲阳侯。
半道逢吴姬,
卷帘出揶揄。
我忆君到此,
不知狂与羞。
一月一见君,
三杯便回桡。
舍舟共连袂,
行上南渡桥。
兴发歌绿水,
秦客为之摇。
鸡鸣复相招,

清宴逸云霄。
赠我数百字,
字字凌风飙。
系之衣裘上,
相忆每长谣。

Playing with the Crescent on Sun's Tower East of Gold Hill, Singing till Dawn and Rowing Drunk with a Few Drinkers in the Ch'inhuai River at Dusk in Purple Fur and Black Gauze Turban and Then Visiting Ts'ui, the Royal Servant, at Stone Town

Last night with the crescent I played;
O'er West Town hung the disc of jade.
Morn sees me buy wine in Gold Hill
And atop Sun's Tower there we trill.
To me occurs he in a silk coat,
So to Stone there we row our boat.
His black gauze scarf so loosely worn,
And his purple fur upside down.
Ashore, he claps to laugh and shout;
Is he the immortal? I doubt.
A dozen drinkers, we're so glad;
Downstream we cheer and drink like mad.
Of other boatmen we make fun
And o'erride Lord Sun, the drowned one.
Midway we meet with a Wu skirt,
And roll up the curtain to flirt.

Your manner I recall, ha, ha!
You don't know what craze and shame are!
One month I see you once, no more;
But three cups drunk, backward you oar.
Now we stop and the boat we leave,
Then get on South Bridge sleeve by sleeve.
O glee, we sing to the flow blue;
A boatman offers now to row.
At dawn each other we invite
To wine that we drink to clouds white.
I'm given a few hundred words
That can fly higher than magic birds.
Inside my fur I'll hide your verse;
I'll chant it, as to me occurs.

* Gold Hill: referring to Nanking, one of the most well-known ancient cities in China, a strategic fort as a gateway to the sea, which has been the capital of Wu, Chin, and many other states or kingdoms, such as the six empires called Six Dynasties and has flourished immensely with increasing trade and travel.
* the immortal: referring to Huichih Wang (A.D. 338 – A.D. 386), a renowned calligrapher with a carefree attitude in the Eastern Chin dynasty. He once took a boat to visit his friend on a whim on a winter evening.
* Lord Sun: a legendary figure. As is said, he threw himself to a river out of guilt, which aroused huge waves.

江上答崔宣城

太华三芙蓉,
明星玉女峰。
寻仙下西岳,
陶令忽相逢。
问我将何事,
湍波历几重?
貂裘非季子,
鹤氅似王恭。
谬忝燕台召,
而陪郭隗踪。
水流知入海,
云去或从龙。
树绕芦洲月,
山鸣鹊镇钟。
还期如叩访,
台岭荫长松。

In Reply to Ts'ui, Magistrate of Hsuan

Mt. Great Flower has three summits high:
Bright Star, Jade Girl and Lotus shy.
To find Void I climb down Mt. West,
And meet with a T'ao, my friend best.
You ask me what I rush to do,
Skipping waves on waves so blue.
No lobbyist marten coat I wear,

But a hermit crane cloak so rare.
I once climbed onto Golden Mound
And followed K'ui Kuo all around.
A stream into the ocean flows;
A cloud floats with the dragon close.
The trees reach the moon o'er Reed Shoal;
The hills strike Magpie Bell to toll.
Should I meet you again someday,
On Mt. Stage with the pines we'll stay.

* Hsuan: an ancient town in present-day Hsuan, Anhui Province.
* Mt. Great Flower: or Mt. Flora, one of the Five Mountains in China, located in Sha'anhsi Province, along with Mt. Ever in Shanhsi, Mt. Arch in Shantung, Mt. Scale in Hunan, and Mt. Tower in Honan.
* Bright Star, Jade Girl and Lotus: three peaks on Mt. Great Flower.
* Void: the state of nature. According to *The Word and the World*, "The Word is void." "Void, it's used without end; moved, the more it will send."
* Mt. West: alias Mt. Great Flower or Mt. Flora.
* a T'ao: a metaphor for Magistrate of Hsuan, a happy person like Poolbright T'ao.
* marten: a weasel-like fur-bearing carnivorous animal (genus *Martes*) having arboreal habits as the pine marten and the large sturdy fisher marten; also the fur of a marten used for the making of expensive clothing.
* Golden Mound: a mound built by King Glare of Yan in order to attract talents to his state.
* K'ui Kuo: K'ui Kuo (A.D. 351 – A.D. 297), a minister and sage in Yan in the Warring States period. He built Golden Mound to attract talents and then Yan grew stronger.
* Magpie: a town in Hsuan. In the Spring and Autumn period, the Ch'u's troop was defeated by Wu at Magpie.
* Magpie Bell: the town bell in Magpie.
* dragon: a fabulous serpent-like giant winged animal that can change its girth and length, a symbol of benevolence and sovereignty in Chinese culture.
* Reed Shoal: under the Southridge, near Hsuan.
* Mt. Stage: Mt. Heaven Stage north of Heaven Stage (Tient'ai) in today's Chechiang Province.

答族侄僧中孚赠玉泉仙人掌茶

常闻玉泉山，
山洞多乳窟。
仙鼠如白鸦，
倒悬清溪月。
茗生此中石，
玉泉流不歇。
根柯洒芳津，
采服润肌骨。
丛老卷绿叶，
枝枝相接连。
曝成仙人掌，
似拍洪崖肩。
举世未见之，
其名定谁传。
宗英乃禅伯，
投赠有佳篇。
清镜烛无盐，
顾惭西子妍。
朝坐有馀兴，
长吟播诸天。

In Reply to Chungfu, My Nephew, a Monk, Who Presents Me with Jade Spring Cactus Tea

In the Jade Spring Mountains I hear
There're many stalactite caves there.

The fairy mice are just like crows white,
A-hanging neath the creek moon bright.
Tea trees amid the pebbles grow;
Without cease Jade Spring does there flow.
Their roots reach the ford and stay in,
Which can be cooked to nourish skin.
The leaves shine green on the trees old;
The branches each to each fast hold.
Sunlit, the tea leaves are cactus-like,
As if the crag neck they will strike.
Such tea one has ne'er seen before;
Who can name it for all to store?
Wow, a great Zen master to me,
You give me the best verse and tea.
Your verse, like a bright mirror best,
Reveals both No Salt and Maid West.
At dawn we sit and, chanting, rise
To present the verse to the skies.

* the Jade Spring Mountains: located in present-day Tangyang, Hupei Province, a historical and cultural attraction bristled with many peculiar caves, grotesque rocks and splendid peaks, esteemed as the Crown of Ch'u's Woodland. About five hundred poems themed on the Jade Spring, composed by Pai Li and other poets have been passed on till today.
* tea: an evergreen Asian shrub or small tree (*Thea sinensis*), having a compact head of leathery, toothed leaves and white or pink flowers. The cured leaves of this plant or an infusion of them are used as a beverage. There are four major types of tea in Chinese culture, namely black tea, green tea, dark tea and white tea, and a large variety of subtypes or brands. Tea, first cultivated in China about 4,700 years ago, is a household necessity, as is shown by an idiom: For a family seven things there need to be: firewood, rice, oil, salt, soya sauce, vinegar, and tea.
* Zen Master: an honored master who practices Zen, a kind of performance of quietude in a form of meditation or contemplation. When Sanskrit jana was spread to China, it

was translated as Zan or Zen for this kind of practice.
* No Salt: name of an ugly woman or referring to any ugly woman.
* Maid West: referring to West Maid, one of the most beautiful women in Chinese history. Once a laundry lady in the State of Yüeh, Maid West was selected to be trained in Yüeh's palace, and sent to the King of Wu as a spy. She quickly won the king's affection, making him indulged in her charm. As a result, the State of Wu waned and perished.

酬裴侍御留岫师弹琴见寄

君同鲍明远，
邀彼休上人。
鼓琴乱白雪，
秋变江上春。
瑶草绿未衰，
攀翻寄情亲。
相思两不见，
流泪空盈巾。

In Reply to P'ei, the Royal Servant, Who Plays the Lute

You are like Chao Pao, the man bright;
The Upper Man there you'd invite.
You play the lute to whirl the Snow,
While autumn becomes a spring flow.
The magic grass, not dry, still green,
You'll pick for him, a friend so keen.
You can't see each other you miss;
Your scarves are wet with tears like this.

* Chao Pao: Chao Pao (A.D. 414 – A.D. 466), a litterateur and poet, good at landscape poems.
* the Upper Man: a monk, who conversed with Chao Pao with poems.

张相公出镇荆州,寻除太子詹事,余时流夜郎,行至江夏,与张公相去千里,公因太府丞王昔使车寄罗衣二事,及五月五日赠余诗,余答以此诗

张衡殊不乐,
应有四愁诗。
惭君锦绣段,
赠我慰相思。
鸿鹄复矫翼,
凤凰忆故池。
荣乐一如此,
商山老紫芝。

Chang, the Scholar, Is Appointed as Prefect of Chaste and Before Long Becomes Chief Supervisor of Crown Prince When I Reach Riversummer on My Way to Exile in Nightboy, a Thousand *Li* from Premier Chang and I Present This Verse to Him on the Fifth Day of the Fifth Moon to Express My Gratitude for His Sending Me a Silk Gown Together with a Verse by a Cart Sent by Hsi Wang, a Grand Hall Manager

You may see Heng Chang's sad, sad eyes;
He wrote for his beauty *Four Sighs*.
I'm shy with your gift of brocade,
So my missing can be repaid.
The wild goose lifts its wings, behold;

The phoenix recalls her pool old.
Honor or pleasure is but such;
Uphill, magic grass we'll pick much.

* Chaste: a geographical region including areas of present-day Hupei and Hunan.
* Nightboy: once the biggest kingdom founded by southern barbarians in the malarial southwest existing from the Warring States period to the Han dynasty. When a Han envoy visited Nigthboy, the king asked: "Which is bigger, Nigthboy or Han?" This self-important question has been a laughing stock ever since. In 27 B.C., Nightboy was wiped out by Han and was made a county.
* Heng Chang: Heng Chang (A.D. 78 - A.D. 139), a great astronomer, mathematician, inventor, geographer, and litterateur in the Eastern Han dynasty, who invented armillary sphere and seismoscope. He felt sad about the waning country and wrote a poem *Four Sighs* to convey his depression.
* *Four Sighs*: the poem Heng Chang wrote when he was unhappy.
* wild goose: an undomesticated goose that is caring and responsible, taken as a symbol of benevolence, righteousness, good manner, wisdom, and faith in Chinese culture.
* phoenix: In Chinese myths, phoenixes, auspicious birds, unlike ordinary ones, only perch on parasol trees, and only eat bamboo shoots and pearly stone.

醉后答丁十八以诗讥余捶碎黄鹤楼

黄鹤高楼已捶碎，
黄鹤仙人无所依。
黄鹤上天诉玉帝，
却放黄鹤江南归。
神明太守再雕饰，
新图粉壁还芳菲。
一州笑我为狂客，
少年往往来相讥。
君平帘下谁家子，
云是辽东丁令威。
作诗调我惊逸兴，
白云绕笔窗前飞。
待取明朝酒醒罢，
与君烂漫寻春晖。

In Reply to Ting Eighteen, Who Sneers at Me, Accusing Me of Smashing Yellow Crane Tower When I'm Drunk

Smashed into bits Yellow Crane Tower has been;
Yellow Crane Hermit has nowhere to lean.
To Lord Jade, Yellow Crane a suit does file;
Yellow Crane is sent south into exile.
Divine Magistrate rebuilds the great tower;
The painted white wall smells like a sweet flower.
I'm laughed at by all the folks in the town;

E'en ridiculed by you, a boy, a clown.
Whose son you are I have asked Master Yan;
Your forebear's Ting from East Liao, a great man.
You should make fun of me, what a surprise!
Your writing brush before the window flies.
When I sober up tomorrow, I'll write
So you can find what's brilliant and what's bright.

* Yellow Crane Tower: a famous ancient tower built by Wu in A.D. 223, located on the top of Mt. Snake, overlooking the Long River, one of the three historical attractions (the other two being Shine River Pavilion and the Old Lute Platform) of today's Wuhan, Hupei Province.
* Yellow Crane Hermit: referring to Ee Fei (? - A.D. 253), one of the Four Sages of Shu in the Three Kingdoms period, an immortal who rode a yellow crane and rested on the tower.
* Lord Jade: also known as the Jade Emperor, the ruler of Heaven and earth according to Wordist mythology.
* Divine Magistrate: referring to Pa Huang (130 B.C.- 51 B.C.), a magistrate of Ying Stream in the Western Han dynasty. He was deified for his merits.
* Master Yan: referring to You Peace (86 B.C.- A.D. 10), a Wordist scholar and thinker at the end of the Western Han dynasty. He lived in seclusion by telling fortune in Silkton (Ch'engtu), and usually guided people to do good based on their potential, advocated the Wordist classic, *The Word and the World*, to benefit the people.
* East Liao: referring to Lingwei Ting, an immortal admired by Wordists. He was born in the east of Liao and transformed himself into a fairy crane and became immortal.
* writing brush: any of various writing brushes or called Chinese brush, widely used for writing or painting, invented or renovated by Tien Meng (259 B.C.- 210 B.C.), a general in the Ch'in dynasty.

答裴侍御先行至石头驿以书见招，期月满泛洞庭

君至石头驿，
寄书黄鹤楼。
开缄识远意，
速此南行舟。
风水无定准，
湍波或滞留。
忆昨新月生，
西檐若琼钩。
今来何所似，
破镜悬清秋。
恨不三五明，
平湖泛澄流。
此欢竟莫遂，
狂杀王子猷。
巴陵定遥远，
持赠解人忧。

In Reply to P'ei, the Royal Servant, Who Arrives at Stone Station and Writes Me an Invitation to Boating on Lake Cavehall on a Full Moon

You reach Stone Station, there remain,
And write to me at Yellow Crane.
Now your invitation I know,

All too soon to South Land I row.

The currents are not smooth at all;

The whirlpools do cause me to stall.

The new moon appeared yestereve,

Like a jade hook o'er the west eave.

Where now, what is it like today?

A mirror in the Milky Way.

Phew, it does not so often glow;

Why not on the lake chase a flow?

We couldn't have fun, not so glad;

We can't, like the hermit, go mad.

Though the Paridge is far away,

Now comfort me your letter may.

* Stone Station: on the west bank of the Yüchang River, i.e. the Kan River today.
* Lake Cavehall: a large lake with an area of 2,740 square kilometers, a lake of strategic importance since ancient times, a place of many resources for today's Hunan Province.
* Yellow Crane: referring to Yellow Crane Tower, a tower built by Wu in A.D. 223, located on the top of Mt. Snake, overlooking the Long River, one of the three historical attractions (the other two being Shine River Pavilion and the Old Lute Platform) of today's Wuhan, Hupei Province.
* the Milky Way: the Silver River in Chinese mythology, a luminous band circling the heavens composed of stars and nebulae; the Galaxy.
* the hermit: referring to Huichih Wang (A.D. 338 - A.D. 386), a renowned calligrapher like his father Hsichih Wang, with a carefree attitude in the Eastern Chin dynasty. He once took a boat to visit his friend on a whim on a winter evening.
* Paridge: the ancient name of Yüehshine, where Emperor Civil of Han was buried.

答高山人兼呈权顾二侯

虹霓掩天光,
哲后起康济。
应运生夔龙,
开元扫氛翳。
太微廓金镜,
端拱清遐裔。
轻尘集嵩岳,
虚点盛明意。
谬挥紫泥诏,
献纳青云际。
谗惑英主心,
恩疏佞臣计。
彷徨庭阙下,
叹息光阴逝。
未作仲宣诗,
先流贾生涕。
挂帆秋江上,
不为云罗制。
山海向东倾,
百川无尽势。
我于鸱夷子,
相去千馀岁。
运阔英达稀,
同风遥执袂。
登舻望远水,
忽见沧浪枻。
高士何处来,

虚舟渺安系。
衣貌本淳古，
文章多佳丽。
延引故乡人，
风义未沦替。
顾侯达语默，
权子识通蔽。
曾是无心云，
俱为此留滞。
双萍易飘转，
独鹤思凌厉。
明晨去潇湘，
共谒苍梧帝。

In Reply to Kao, the Hermit, and Also to Ch'üan and Ku

A rainbow does eclipse the sun;
A wise lord helps commons as one.
Good luck sees Uni-Dragon leap;
All begun does fog and haze sweep.
O'er the throne Gold Mirror appears;
Inaction or freedom now clears.
Light dust does gather on Mt. Tower;
As lenient is He, who holds power.
But purple decrees they misuse
And remonstrances they abuse.
They disturb His Majesty's heart;
All courtiers, confused, stay apart.
By the court I pace up and down;

Time elapses fast to my frown.
Before I can a verse compose,
My tears keep dripping down my nose.
On the chill river I'll set sail,
For all thick haze that does prevail.
The hills and seas eastward descend;
All the rivers flow without end.
It's been a thousand years and more
Since Li Fan withdrew to the shore.
The way is broad but talents few;
May a confidant come into view.
On board I look afar, look more;
Following the waves comes an oar!
Where does the hermit come from, where?
He anchors his boat over there.
He looks simple, so simply dressed;
But his verse is good, of a crest.
He talks with me about his town;
There, good virtues have not come down.
The herald, a sign, needs not say;
The plotter, well-thought, knows the way.
A heartless cloud I used to be;
Now all troubles here trouble me.
Two duckweeds can turn fast around;
A single crane thinks so profound.
Tomorrow, we'll start for the ford
To worship Hibiscus, our Lord.

* Uni-Dragon: referring to Unilimb and Dragon, a dyad of Hibiscus's ministers, one in charge of music and the other responsible for remonstrance. Ancients were usually named after flora and fauna, such like Snake, Worm, Elephant and so on. Unilimb, a

legendary one-limb monster, and dragon, a mythical reptile-like monster, were used as names in ancient China.
* Allbegun: Allbegun (A.D. 713 – A.D. 741), the reign title of Emperor Deepsire of T'ang. Allbegun is the most flourishing and powerful period of the T'ang Empire.
* Gold Mirror: implying the right way.
* Mt. Tower: located in the west of present-day Honan Province, one of the Five Sacred Mountains in China and an important theme of Chinese culture. It is one of the five sanctuaries of Wordism, and the abode of God of Mt. Tower worshipped by Han Chinese, with an area of 450 square kilometers, consisting of Mt. Greatroom and Mt. Smallroom, having 72 peaks, 350 meters above sea level at the lowest and 1,512 meters at the highest.
* Li Fan: Li Fan (536 B.C.– 448 B.C.), a renowned statesman, strategist, economist and Wordist in the Spring and Autumn period. Fan changed his name to live in seclusion after he helped the State of Yüeh wipe out Wu.
* duckweed: any of several small, disk-shaped, floating aquatic plants common in streams and ponds.
* Hibiscus: Shun if transliterated, an ancient sovereign, a descendant of Lord Yellow, regarded as one of Five Lords in prehistoric China.

答杜秀才五松见赠

昔献长杨赋,
天开云雨欢。
当时待诏承明里,
皆道扬雄才可观。
敕赐飞龙二天马,
黄金络头白玉鞍。
浮云蔽日去不返,
总为秋风摧紫兰。
角巾东出商山道,
采秀行歌咏芝草。
路逢园绮笑向人,
两君解来一何好。
闻道金陵龙虎盘,
还同谢朓望长安。
千峰夹水向秋浦,
五松名山当夏寒。
铜井炎炉歊九天,
赫如铸鼎荆山前。
陶公矍铄呵赤电,
回禄睢盱扬紫烟。
此中岂是久留处,
便欲烧丹从列仙。
爱听松风且高卧,
飕飕吹尽炎氛过。
登崖独立望九州,
阳春欲奏谁相和?
闻君往年游锦城,

章仇尚书倒屣迎。
飞笺络绎奏明主,
天书降问回恩荣。
肮脏不能就珪组,
至今空扬高蹈名。
夫子工文绝世奇,
五松新作天下推。
吾非谢尚邀彦伯,
异代风流各一时。
一时相逢乐在今,
袖拂白云开素琴,
弹为三峡流泉音。
从兹一别武陵去,
去后桃花春水深。

In Reply to Tu, the Showcharm Who Writes Me a Poem at Mt. Five Pines

I wrote *Tall Poplar* for the Lord;
My heart amid clouds and rain soared.
A recruit, in Lighting Hall saw me wait,
Acclaimed for my flair, as Man Yang's as great.
I was granted two Pegasuses bold,
With jade white saddles and harnesses gold.
Then dark clouds veiling the sun will not go,
And to the violets a high wind does blow.
Wearing a scarf, I go east along Shang Pass,
Singing and picking blooms and magic grass.
A passer-by smiles: You're one of the Four
And asks me if I'm as well as before.

Gold Hill hides dragons and tigers, he says,
Where with Hsieh one can at Capital gaze.
Mt. Autumn River Shoal hugs the clear pool;
Mt. Five Pines even in summer keeps cool.
The bronze mine sees forges on fire, so hot;
Like Lord Yellow cast wares, tripod or pot.
Lord T'ao, hale and hearty, Firefiend does poke;
Fire God, cheerful, gleeful, spreads purple smoke.
It's not somewhere one can for long stay;
It's where elixir is made for the Way.
I would listen to pines while lying there
And hear a sough blowing off a hot air.
Standing on the Cliff, I o'erlook the land.
I'd play *Spring and Snow*; who can understand?
I hear you toured Silkton, Lotus Town called;
The minister welcomed you, so enthralled.
He wrote to Lord and did you recommend;
His Majesty did to you His grace send.
But you declined the appointment with pride,
And now your great name is spread far and wide.
Your elegance does the whole world outrun;
Your piece Five Pines is praised by everyone.
If I claim we're Muses, I dare not boast;
But the age we lead, and the stage we host.
Now we meet, we should be happy today;
Set the zither and sweep the clouds away,
And the *Three Gorges Fountain Spring* we play.
Now I'm leaving for Fairyland alone;
The spring pool is deep, with peach blossoms strewn.

* showcharm: a talent recommended for official use through imperial civil-service

examinations or a well-learned person in ancient China.
* Mt. Five Pines: a mountain in present-day Copperridge (Tungling), Anhui Province.
* *Tall Poplar Prose*: a verse written by Man Yang, a great scholar in the Han dynasty.
* Lighting Hall: an imperial palace in the Han dynasty.
* Man Yang: Man Yang (53 B.C.- A.D. 18), Hsiung Yang if transliterated, a great scholar, rhymed prose writer and official in the Han dynasty. His *The Great One* is a masterpiece, a literary genre between verse and prose, which can be termed as euph (a coinage based on euphuism and euphemism); it has had a deep influence on works of later generations. According to *History of the Han Dynasty*, when other officials flattered those in power, only Man Yang kept to himself to write his philosophical work, *The Great One*.
* Pegasuses: fine horses from the west. According to the regulation in the T'ang dynasty, when a scholar is called to the imperial academy, he would be given a fine horse.
* Shang Pass: When Ch'in met its peril, the Four Grey Heads escaped to the deep of Mt. Shang through this pass and waited for the the country to be pacified.
* one of the Four: referring to four Wordist hermits living at Mt. Shang. They were invited a think tank for the House of Han.
* Gold Hill: referring to Nanking, one of the most well-known ancient capitals in China.
* Hsieh: referring to T'iao Hsieh (A.D. 464 - A.D. 499), an outstanding highborn landscape poet.
* Lord Yellow: alias Cartshaft, the first of the five heavenly gods in myth and the earliest ancestor of Chinese people. It was said that Lord Yellow made a tripod in the Chaste Hills. As the tripod was done, a dragon came down to visit him. He and his 70 or more officials and consorts all rode on the dragon and flew to the sky. In myth, when Lord Yellow and his retinue rode the dragon away, they left some junior officials on earth, who could but pull the dragon's beard in vain. All they got was only a strand of beard and the sword dropped from Lord Yellow.
* tripod: a cooking utensil or cauldron with three feet or legs, usually cast with bronze, popular in ancient China, a symbol of a powerful family.
* Lord T'ao: an alchemist in the Han dynasty. When he was refining metal, a flash of purple light burst and Fire God showed up to tell him there would be a red dragon picking him up to heaven.
* *Spring and Snow*: an ancient song that represents high-brow sophisticated arts.
* Silkton: the other name of Ch'engtu for it was a town of silk.
* Three Gorges: referring to three gorges of the Willow River in the west of Chechiang.
* *Three Gorges Fountain Spring*: a Han Conservatoire verse compiled by Hsien Ruan in

the Chin dynasty.
* Fairyland: indicating Peach Blossom Source, a perfect seclusion written by Poolbright T'ao.

至陵阳山登天柱石酬韩侍御见招隐黄山

韩众骑白鹿,
西往华山中。
玉女千馀人,
相随在云空。
见我传秘诀,
精诚与天通。
何意到陵阳,
游目送飞鸿。
天子昔避狄,
与君亦乘骢。
拥兵五陵下,
长策遏胡戎。
时泰解绣衣,
脱身若飞蓬。
鸾凤翻羽翼,
啄粟坐樊笼。
海鹤一笑之,
思归向辽东。
黄山过石柱,
巘崿上攒丛。
因巢翠玉树,
忽见浮丘公。
又引王子乔,
吹笙舞松风。
朗咏紫霞篇,
请开蕊珠宫。

步纲绕碧落,
倚树招青童。
何日可携手,
遗形入无穷。

Climbing Heavenly Crag on Mt. Ridgeshine to Thank Han, the Royal Servant, Who Has Invited Me to Mt. Yellow

Mister Han, a white deer you ride
To Flora and there you'll abide.
Lo, one thousand girls, what a crowd,
They follow you who're like a cloud.
I have a secret knack for you,
Which is as staunch as the sky blue.
Do come to Ridgeshine as you please;
I'll see you off like the wild geese.
The Lord who would barbarians shun
Rode a piebald with you to run.
The Fifth Ridge saw you troops command
To check the Huns out of the land.
When you took off your silken gown,
It seemed to fly like thistledown.
A phoenix flaps with a free mind;
A warbler's to its cage confined.
The seagull spreads its wings with a smile;
It'll go back to East Liao this while.
O'er crags on Mt. Yellow it flies;
The rocks on rocks will reach the skies.
When it'll perch on a jadeite tree,

Mister Floating Knoll it does see.
And there arrives Crown Prince High now,
Who plays the flute to the pine sough.
The Purple Clouds he does recite;
Please open Pistil Pearl so bright.
There the hanging track in the air,
He greets Green Boy by the tree there.
When can we go out hand in hand
To tour the void and boundless land?

* white deer: a Wordist symbol often seen in Chinese paintings: the animal ridden by an immortal.
* Flora: referring to Mt. Flora, one of the Five Mountains in China, regarded as the steepest and saintly mountain in China as it is one of the progenitors of Chinese culture, the shrine of Wordism and the abode of God of Mt. Flora, located in today's Flowershade, Sha'ahsi Province.
* Ridgeshine: Lingyang if transliterated, a county located in present-day Anhui Province. According to legend, Sir Glare became immortal on the way to Mt. Ridgeshine.
* wild goose: an undomesticated goose that is caring and responsible, taken as a symbol of benevolence, righteousness, good manner, wisdom, and faith in Chinese culture.
* the Fifth Ridge: indicating mausoleums of five emperors in the T'ang dynasty.
* thistledown: the pappus of a thistle; the ripe silky fibers from the dry flower of a thistle, a metaphor for drifting or wandering.
* phoenix: In Chinese myths, phoenixes, auspicious birds, unlike ordinary ones, only perch on parasol trees, and only eat bamboo shoots and pearly stone.
* seagull: a kind of sea bird, any gull or large tern, a symbol of clean integrity. The seagulls in the Wordist book *Sir Line* (Liehtzu) are particularly sensitive to impurity of motive and will make friends only with the completely guileless and disinterested.
* East Liao: an area east of the Liao River and north of East Sea, about 500 square kilometers.
* Mt. Yellow: located in Anhui Province. Mt. Yellow is one of the most famous mountains in China with natural, literary, and cultural attractions, featured with wondrous pines, clouds and hotsprings. It is said that Lord Yellow used to make elixirs here.

- * Mister Floating Knoll: a legendary immortal.
- * Crown Prince High: referring to Prince of Front (567 B.C.-549 B.C.), the first son of King Spirit of Chough. He was an intelligent and courageous young man. Though high as a prince, he had few desires and was keen on the flute and the Word. As legend goes, he met Mister Floating Knoll, followed him to deep mountains, and rose to be immortal after his early death.
- * *The Purple Clouds*: a Wordist book.
- * Pistil Pearl: a fairy palace in Wordist myths.
- * Green Boy: an immortal living in East Sea.

酬崔十五见招

尔有鸟迹书,
相招琴溪饮。
手迹尺素中,
如天落云锦。
读罢向空笑,
疑君在我前。
长吟字不灭,
怀袖且三年。

To Ts'ui Fifteen, Who Gives Me a Treat

The bird footprint script you can write,
Let's drink by the Lute Stream, all right?
On white cloth now you run your hand,
The words, like clouds that fall to land,
You, reading, laugh towards the skies,
As though you're just before my eyes.
Chant long lest the book disappears;
Keep it in your sleeve for three years.

* bird footprint script: Chinese characters looking like birds' footprints, invented by Lord Yellow's histographer Ts'angchieh, who designed Chinese characters, observing the Heaven and overlooking the earth to find out how things moved and worked.
* the Lute Stream: a stream in present-day Anhui. It's said that there was a man named Ch'in Kao from Chao in the Chough dynasty good at playing the lute, and he became immortal at the stream, hence the name.

答王十二寒夜独酌有怀

昨夜吴中雪,
子猷佳兴发。
万里浮云卷碧山,
青天中道流孤月。
孤月沧浪河汉清,
北斗错落长庚明。
怀余对酒夜霜白,
玉床金井冰峥嵘。
人生飘忽百年内,
且须酣畅万古情。
君不能狸膏金距学斗鸡,
坐令鼻息吹虹霓。
君不能学哥舒,
横行青海夜带刀,
西屠石堡取紫袍。
吟诗作赋北窗里,
万言不直一杯水。
世人闻此皆掉头,
有如东风射马耳。
鱼目亦笑我,
谓与明月同。
骅骝拳跼不能食,
蹇驴得志鸣春风。
折杨黄华合流俗,
晋君听琴枉清角。
巴人谁肯和阳春,
楚地由来贱奇璞。

黄金散尽交不成，
白首为儒身被轻。
一谈一笑失颜色，
苍蝇贝锦喧谤声。
曾参岂是杀人者？
谗言三及慈母惊。
与君论心握君手，
荣辱于余亦何有？
孔圣犹闻伤凤麟，
董龙更是何鸡狗！
一生傲岸苦不谐，
恩疏媒劳志多乖。
严陵高揖汉天子，
何必长剑拄颐事玉阶。
达亦不足贵，
穷亦不足悲。
韩信羞将绛灌比，
祢衡耻逐屠沽儿。
君不见李北海，
英风豪气今何在！
君不见裴尚书，
土坟三尺蒿棘居！
少年早欲五湖去，
见此弥将钟鼎疏。

In Reply to Wang Twelve, Who Drinks Alone at Night

Last night in Mid-Wu it did snow；
So drunk, you were mad like Tsu-yu.

The boundless clouds hang o'er the mountains high;
The moon seems to flow across the blue sky.
The Milky Way clear, the moon lonely flows;
The Dippers dispersed, Venus brightly glows
The night frost beaten, for me you drank wine,
While the well and rail were ice bound to shine.
Life's within a hundred years, come and go;
Let's drink up to discharge our age-old woe.
You should not hail cockfights, cocks greased and in gold claw mail
Or from your nose to a rainbow exhale.
You should not learn from Han Koshu,
Who in Bluesea robbed and killed up and down
And looted Stone Castle for a purple gown.
By your north window you may chant and write;
Your long appeal's not worth a sip or bite.
Hearing such a thing all people will veer,
Like east wind blowing o'er your horse's ear.
The dried fish eyes sneer at me, too,
Saying they're the same as pearls true.
The swift horse now hunched can't eat or can't neigh;
The lame ass, fulfilled, to spring wind, does bray.
Willow Sprays and *Yellow Buds* suit vogue taste,
To Lord of Chin, *Attic* is but a waste.
How can vulgar Pas *White Snow* praise or prize?
As always Ch'u folks best crude jade despise.
One may spend all gold but no friends come on;
A gray haired scholar is looked down upon.
Talking and laughing, he turns about, stern,
He's like a blowfly that a shell does spurn.
How could Tseng a murderer be, alack;
The slander took his kind mother aback.

Now we talk hand in hand and heart to heart;
How can shame or honor anything start?
Confucius deplored the Unicorn then;
Tung Lung was cheap, only a dog or hen!
So haughty I am, so all life I fail;
His Grace lost, efforts come to no avail.
Light Yan, aloft, refused to serve Han's Lord,
How should I serve the crown, hanging my sword?
With success you need not feel glad;
For poorness you should not be sad.
To be with Chou or Kuan Hsin Han did hate;
Scale Mi felt ashamed to be T'u-Ku's mate.
Don't you see North Sea Li,
Where is his valiance, and where can it be?
Don't you see Premier P'ei,
His tomb's rank with weeds and in weeds does stay.
When young in the Five Lakes I wished to oar;
Now I'd reject bells and robes all the more.

* Tsu-yu: referring to Huichih Wang (A.D. 338 – A.D. 386), a renowned calligrapher with a carefree attitude in the Eastern Chin dynasty, Tsu-yu by courtesy name. He once took a boat to visit his friend on a whim on a winter evening.
* the Milky Way: a luminous band circling the heavens composed of stars and nebulae; the Galaxy.
* the Dippers: the Big Dipper and the Little Dipper.
* cockfight: the game of cockfighting. Cockfighting has a long history in China, a main recreational activity all through history. The earliest cockfighting in China recorded in *Historical Records* was in 770 B.C.
* Han Koshu: a senior commander in the T'ang dynasty, descended on his father's side from Turgash chieftains and on his mother's from a well-known Khotanese family.
* Bluesea: an area in the west of China, present-day Ch'inghai Province.
* Stone Castle: a district in Kansu.
* purple gown: implying a senior position. The T'ang rules stipulated that officials of the

third grade and above wear purple gowns.
* fish eye: a metaphor for something cheap or fake, especially when collocated with "pearl", for example, "pass fish eyes for pearls" means "mix the genuine with the fake".
* *Willow Sprays* and *Yellow Buds*: vulgar songs in the ancient times.
* *Attic*: an elegant song which was said that it could only be played for man of virtue otherwise the listener would get unlucky. Lord Peace of Chin forced Master K'uang, a musician, to play the song for him, which resulted in three years' drought in Chin and an illness that struck the lord.
* Pas: vulgar people in the ancient times, people of the State of Pa near the State of Shu.
* *White Snow*: an elegant high-brow song in the ancient times, which few could understand.
* Ch'u folks best crude jade despise: indicating the story that Ho Pien presented crude jade stone he found to monarchs of Ch'u but failed twice. Ho held the jade stone crying bitterly for the previous misjudgment. Up to this point, the precious jade was finally appreciated by the new lord.
* Tseng: referring to Sen Tseng (505 B.C.- 435 B.C.), one of Confucius' students, a representative of Confucianism. It's said a man who had the same name as Tseng killed a person. Others told his mother that Tseng committed murder, but his mother did not believe it. As the mother was told the third time, she vacillated over the rumour.
* Confucius deplored the Unicorn: A unicorn was considered as a divine and benevolent creature in legends. Lord Sad of Lu and his officials once captured a unicorn but none of them recognized it. They brought it to Confucius and he wept for the scared creature, thinking it was a sign for a hard age.
* Tung Lung (? - A.D. 357): a courtier in the Sixteen Kingdoms period.
* Light Yan: referring to Tsuling Yan (39 B.C.- A.D. 41) if transliterated, a renowned hermit in the Han dynasty. He showed his talent at an early age. After Hsiu Liu was enthroned to be the emperor of Han, Yan was invited several times to serve the court. Though the emperor was an acquaintance of his, Yan declined the offer and chose to live in seclusion in the Richspring Hills.
* Chou or Kuan: referring to Po Chou (? - 169 B.C.) and Ying Kuan (? - 176 B.C.), founding commanders of Han.
* Hsin Han: a founding commander of the Han regime. He had been poor and shown a good endurance of humiliation. Once a young man made fun of him and forced him to crawl through his legs, and Han did so without changing his expression. When he was not appreciated in pursuit of an official career or good at doing business, Han used to rely on an elder laundry woman who pitied him and gave him food without expectation

of a return.
* Scale Mi: Heng Mi (A.D. 173 – A.D. 198) if transliterated, a verse writer and upright man in the Three Kingdoms period. When people asked him why he did not join Ch'un Chen and Lang Ssuma, highborn statesmen of Wei, Scale Mi, proud as he was, said he did not want to be with men of humble origin.
* T'u-Ku: a contemptuous appellation for man of humble origin. T'u (butcher) and Ku (alcohol seller) both were considered low-ranked occupations in the ancient times.
* North Sea Li: referring to Yung Li (A.D. 678 – A.D. 747), an official and calligrapher in the T'ang dynasty. He was once prefect of North Sea, today's Ch'ingchow, Shantung Province. He was killed by Premier Linfu Li out of schemes and intrigues.
* Premier P'ei: referring to Tunfu P'ei (? – A.D. 747), a minister of penalty in the T'ang dynasty. North Sea Li and Premier P'ei were both talented men but were murdered by Linfu Li (A.D. 683 – A.D. 753), a treacherous premier.
* the Five Lakes: referring to Lake T'ai and the other four lakes around. As legend goes, Li Fan (536 B.C.– 448 B.C.), a renowned statesman, strategist, economist and Wordist in the Spring and Autumn period, changed his name to live in seclusion among the Five Lakes after he helped the State of Yüeh wipe out Wu.

古近体诗六十首
Old-new Rhythmic Poetry, 60 Poems

游南阳白水登石激作

朝涉白水源，
暂与人俗疏。
岛屿佳境色，
江天涵清虚。
目送去海云，
心闲游川鱼。
长歌尽落日，
乘月归田庐。

Touring White Water Source in Southshine

At dawn White Water Source I wade,
Out of the dust world of dust made.
The isle's the best sight of the brine;
The sea and sky form a void sign.
I see off white clouds off the sea;
My heart swims with the fish, so free.
I sing for long to the setting sun;
And go back home with moonlight on.

* White Water Source: a river located in Southshine, Honan.
* Southshine: an alternative name for South Town, which had nurtured the Five Sages of Southshine: Great Grand, Sage of Wisdom in the Shang and Chough dynasties, Li Fan (536 B.C.- 448 B.C.), Sage of Commerce in the Spring and Autumn period, Heng Chang (A.D. 78 - A.D. 139), Sage of Science in the Eastern Han dynasty, Chungching Chang, Sage of Medicine in the Eastern Han dynasty, and Bright Chuke (A.D. 181 - A.D. 234), Sage of Strategy in the Eastern Han dynasty.

游南阳清泠泉

惜彼落日暮,
爱此寒泉清。
西辉逐流水,
荡漾游子情。
空歌望云月,
曲尽长松声。

Touring the Cold Spring in Southshine

I'd hold fast to the setting sun;
I linger there with Cold Spring's run.
The glimmer west the waves does chase;
The rippling flow my heart does raise.
I sing to the cloud and moon now
While the pine trees breathe out a sough.

* Cold Spring: a spring under Mt. Rich, 15 kilometers from Southshine.
* Southshine: an alternative name for South Town, which had nurtured the Five Sages of Southshine: Great Grand, Sage of Wisdom in the Shang and Chough dynasties, Li Fan (536 B.C.- 448 B.C.), Sage of Commerce in the Spring and Autumn period, Heng Chang (A.D. 78 - A.D. 139), Sage of Science in the Eastern Han dynasty, Chungching Chang, Sage of Medicine in the Eastern Han dynasty, and Bright Chuke (A.D. 181 - A.D. 234), Sage of Strategy in the Eastern Han dynasty.
* the moon: the planet of the earth, which appears at night and gives off shining silvery light, an image of purity and solitude in Chinese culture.

寻鲁城北范居士失道落苍耳中见范置酒摘苍耳作

雁度秋色远,
日静无云时。
客心不自得,
浩漫将何之?
忽忆范野人,
闲园养幽姿。
茫然起逸兴,
但恐行来迟。
城壕失往路,
马首迷荒陂。
不惜翠云裘,
遂为苍耳欺。
入门且一笑,
把臂君为谁。
酒客爱秋蔬,
山盘荐霜梨。
他筵不下箸,
此席忘朝饥。
酸枣垂北郭,
寒瓜蔓东篱。
还倾四五酌,
自咏猛虎词。
近作十日欢,
远为千载期。
风流自簸荡,
谑浪偏相宜。

酣来上马去，
却笑高阳池。

On My Way to Visit Fan, the Hermit, I Go Astray and Fall into Cocklebur and Then I Meet with Him, Who Treats Me with Wine and Picks Cocklebur off Me

Wild geese fly thru the autumn hue,
So silent, no clouds in the blue.
I wander out for long, distressed;
Drifting, driven, where can I rest?
Fan suddenly occurs to me;
He's raising orchids there, so free.
My interest's so highly raised
That to his garden I make haste.
Nearby the moat I lose my way;
In the wild e'en a horse may stray.
I never mind the cocklebur
That bullies my emerald cloud fur.
He laughs when I enter the door,
Holding my arm, asking: what for?
Wow, autumn greens to go with wine,
And on this plate of pears we dine.
I don't care about others' feast;
With this banquet I feel most pleased.
The north town sees jujubes grow tall;
The east hedge has melon vines sprawl.
Four cups, five cups and more we want;
While drunk, *O Fierce Tiger* we chant.

> For ten days on, drunk we remain;
> An aeon from now, we drink again?
> All gallantry goes with unrest,
> But good humor suits it the best.
> Awake now, I get on my horse
> And laugh: I will be back of course.

* wild goose: an undomesticated goose that is caring and responsible, taken as a symbol of benevolence, righteousness, good manner, wisdom, and faith in Chinese culture.
* orchid: any of a widely distributed family of terrestrial or epiphytic monocotyledonous plants having thickened bulbous roots and often very showy distinctive flowers, one of the four most important floral images in Chinese literature, which are wintersweet, orchid, bamboo, and chrysanthemum.
* cocklebur: a low branching, rank weed (genus *Xanthium*) of the composite family, with hard ovoid or oblong two-celled burs about an inch long.
* jujube: any of a genus of trees or shrubs of the buckthorn family, especially the common jujube, the lotus tree.
* *O Fierce Tiger*: a poem composed Kuanghsi Ch'u, an official and poet in the T'ang dynasty, a representative of Chinese idyllists.

东鲁门泛舟二首
Boating at Gate of East Lu, Two Poems

其 一

日落沙明天倒开，
波摇石动水萦回。
轻舟泛月寻溪转，
疑是山阴雪后来。

No. 1

The sun sinks, the sand shines, the day has dawned;
The waves shake, the stones move, the stream flows round.
My boat in the moonlit stream turns about;
Is he coming from the snow shade? I doubt.

* Is he coming from the snow shade: Pai Li wonders whether he is Huichih Wang, the famous calligrapher, coming from the shady side of a mountain as the latter often lived there.

其 二

水作青龙盘石堤，
桃花夹岸鲁门西。
若教月下乘舟去，
何啻风流到剡溪？

No. 2

Round Stone Dyke water's like a dragon blue;
Peach flowers light the banks west of Gate of Lu.
If you boat there beneath the bright moon beam,
Who can compare with you on the Yan Stream?

* peach: any tree of the genus *Prunus Percica*, blooming brilliantly and bearing fruit, a fleshy, juicy, edible drupe, considered sacred in China, a symbol of romance, prosperity and longevity.
* dragon: a fabulous serpent-like giant winged animal that can change its girth and length, a totem of the Chinese nation, a symbol of benevolence and sovereignty in Chinese culture.
* you: referring to Pai Li himself. Pai Li is asking himself in his reverie.
* the Yan Stream: a main stream with rich cultural attractions in present-day Shengchow, Chechiang Province.

秋猎孟诸夜归置酒单父东楼观妓

倾晖速短炬，
走海无停川。
冀餐圆丘草，
欲以还颓年。
此事不可得，
微生若浮烟。
骏发跨名驹，
雕弓控鸣弦。
鹰豪鲁草白，
狐兔多肥鲜。
邀遮相驰逐，
遂出城东田。
一扫四野空，
喧呼鞍马前。
归来献所获，
炮炙宜霜天。
出舞两美人，
飘飖若云仙。
留欢不知疲，
清晓方来旋。

Returning at Night from Autumn Hunting at Mengchu and Watching Singing Girls at Feast on East Tower in Shanfu

The torch bright burns down from its top;

The stream runs sea-bound without stop.
The hummock grass I wish to eat;
So that my prime I can repeat.
But that is for sure beyond me;
Life so short, smoke it seems to be.
Why not get on my horse, yo ho?
I will go hunting, bent my bow.
Eagles fly above the grass white;
Foxes and hares look fat and bright.
With my friend I'll chase up and down,
Down to the fields east of the town.
All game we will sweep and wipe out;
Before our steeds they shriek and shout.
All our trophies we will amass;
Stew, roast, a good winter to pass!
We may invite two singing girls,
Like fairies, all ogles and swirls.
Let them stay and for them I yearn;
Only at dawn may they return.

* Shanfu: Shan County, a county in present-day Shantung. The place was named after Ch'üan Shan or Shanfu, Hibiscus's teacher, and is known as the birthplace of Empress Lü, Pang Liu's wife, a woman politician of Han.
* eagle: a diurnal bird of prey of the family *Accipitridae* of worldwide distribution, notable for keen sight and strong flight, usually praised as a hero in Chinese culture.
* fox: a burrowing canine mammal (genus *Vulpes*) having a long pointed muzzle and a long bushy tail, commonly reddish-brown in color, characterized by its cunning.
* hare: a rodent (genus *Lepus*) with cleft upper lip, long ears, and long hind legs, characterized by its timidity and swiftness, habitating woodland, farmland or grassland.

游泰山六首
Touring Mt. Arch, Six Poems

其 一

四月上泰山,
石平御道开。
六龙过万壑,
涧谷随萦回。
马迹绕碧峰,
于今满青苔。
飞流洒绝巘,
水急松声哀。
北眺崿嶂奇,
倾崖向东摧。
洞门闭石扇,
地底兴云雷。
登高望蓬流,
想象金银台。
天门一长啸,
万里清风来。
玉女四五人,
飘飖下九垓。
含笑引素手,
遗我流霞杯。
稽首再拜之,
自愧非仙才。
旷然小宇宙,
弃世何悠哉。

No. 1

The fourth moon climb Mt. Arch I will;
The cliff-side Lord's Way runs uphill.
His carts passed all the vales profound;
The rivers turned and turned around.
The hoof prints round peaks on the way
Are covered with green moss today.
The water flies down the crags steep,
Where with a sough the pines do weep.
Gazing north you find peaks abrupt;
The cliffs east leaning will erupt.
The cave is closed behind the door;
From under comes a thunder roar.
On high a fairyland I see,
And Treasure Mound rises to be.
At Heaven's Gate I give a shout;
A breeze from afar comes about.
Behold, the fair girls, four or five,
From Nine Heavens they now arrive.
They extend their hands with a smile;
Their cup for me does me beguile.
I bow to them and bow down twice;
No talent, I can't them entice.
Now, I'm broad, and the cosmos small;
I'll reject the world, reject all.

* Mt. Arch: one of the five especially sacred mountains in China, one for each of the four directions and one at the center. Mt. Arch, in the east in today's Shantung Province, is the most revered of the five, as its name may suggest, and its summit is

the destination of many pilgrims. 72 sovereigns in prehistoric China made sacrifices to the god of the mountain and 12 emperors made sacrifices from the Ch'in dynasty to the Ch'ing dynasty, clearly recorded in history books. Mt. Arch complex includes many lower ridges and summits. The other four mountains are Mt. Ever, west in Shanhsi, Mt. Scale, south in Hunan, Mt. Flora, north in Sha'anhsi, and Mt. Tower, the central one in Honan.

* Lord's Way: a broad way leading to the top of the mountain. A sovereign's cart is drawn by six horses, and escorts' carts have four horses each.
* Fairyland: a legendary ideal abode for immortals, sometimes thought of as being in the middle of East Sea, sometimes high above in the sky.
* Treasure Mound: a platform usually in clouds on Mt. Arch.
* Heaven's Gate: a name shared by many mountains in China. There are three Heaven's Gates on Mt. Arch—First Heaven's Gate, Middle Heaven's Gate, and South Heaven's Gate.
* cosmos: the world or universe considered as a system, perfect in order and arrangement, opposed to chaos.

其 二

清晓骑白鹿,
直上天门山。
山际逢羽人,
方瞳好容颜。
扪萝欲就语,
却掩青云关。
遗我鸟迹书,
飘然落岩间。
其字乃上古,
读之了不闲。
感此三叹息,
从师方未还。

No. 2

The morn sees me a white deer ride
All the way to Mt. Heaven's Gate.
I meet with one at mountainside,
A hermit with eyes bright, so great.
I would speak while a vine I crook,
He enters blue clouds, seen no more.
He left with me a bird script book,
As if dropped to the rock of yore.
The characters are old-aged, and
One can't any script understand.
At this I heave sigh upon sigh;
To learn from the master I'll try.

* white deer: a Wordist symbol often seen in Chinese paintings; the animal ridden by an immortal.
* Mt. Heaven's Gate: unidentified in this poem. There are many mountains bearing the name in China, for example, one in Changchiachieh, Hunan Province, and one in Tangt'u, Anhui Province.
* bird script: also called bird footprint script, Chinese characters looking like birds' footprints, invented by Lord Yellow's histographer Ts'angchieh, who designed Chinese characters, observing the Heaven and overlooking the earth to find out how things moved and worked.

其 三

平明登日观，
举手开云关。
精神四飞扬，
如出天地间。
黄河从西来，
窈窕入远山。
凭崖览八极，
目尽长空闲。
偶然值青童，
绿发双云鬟。
笑我晚学仙，
蹉跎凋朱颜。
踌躇忽不见，
浩荡难追攀。

No. 3

At daybreak I climb Sunview and
Do push aside clouds with my hand.
My spirits soar above and fly
As if to spurt out of the sky.
The Yellow River comes from west
And flows to the hills without rest.
Atop the cliff I look around;
What I see is void and profound.
Into a sage child I now run;
Black haired, he wears a high bun.
He laughs that I've started too late;

I have passed my prime to abate.
He goes away before my eyes;
Where can I find him neath the skies?

* Sunview: referring to Mt. Sunview, the highest peak in the southeast of Mt. Arch, the first of the five most important mountains in China.
* the Yellow River: the second longest river in China, flowing across Loess Plateau, hence yellow water all the way. It is 5,464 kilometers long, with a drainage area of 752,443 square kilometers. It has nurtured the Chinese nation, hence regarded as the cradle of Chinese civilization. As legend goes, the river derived from a yellow dragon that, couchant on Midland Plain, ate yellow soil, flooded crops, devoured people and stock, and was finally tamed by Great Worm, the First King of Hsia (cir. 21 B.C.-16 B.C.).

其 四

清斋三千日，
裂素写道经。
吟诵有所得，
众神卫我形。
云行信长风，
飒若羽翼生。
攀崖上日观，
伏槛窥东溟。
海色动远山，
天鸡已先鸣。
银台出倒景，
白浪翻长鲸。
安得不死药，
高飞向蓬瀛。

No. 4

Three thousand days, I've fasted right;
I'll copy the Word on cloth white.
If I chant for a good yield;
All gods and spirits will me shield.
If all airs and clouds to me blow,
I'll run fast as if two wings grow.
I climb Mt. Sunview and I, wee,
On the railing look at East Sea.
The sea blue moves the distant hills;
The Heaven cock rises and trills.
Silver towers' shade does there prevail;

> The white wave is like a huge whale.
> Where's elixir so one'll not die?
> To Fairyland there I now fly.

* the Word: referring to Tao if transliterated, the most significant and profoundest concept in Chinese philosophy, comparable to the Word in the Bible or Logos in Heraclitus' philosophy. According to Laocius's *The Word and the World*: "The Word is void, but its use is infinite. O deep! It seems to be the root of all things."
* Mt. Sunview: referring to the highest peak in the southeast of Mt. Arch.
* East Sea: what is East China Sea today, not far from Mt. Arch.
* the Heaven cock: In Chinese mythology, a Heaven cock perches on a huge tree whose branches spread 1,500 kilometers wide. When the sun is out and lights up the tree, the Heaven cock will crow, and all cocks in the world will follow.
* whale: a cetaceous mammal of fish-like form, especially one of the larger pelagic species, as distinguished from dolphins and porpoises. Whales have the fore limbs developed as broad flattened paddles, hind limbs absent, and a thick layer of fat or blubber immediately beneath the skin. A whale is a symbol of great ambition, fortitude and uniqueness.
* Fairyland: an imaginary place for immortals, an ideal place free of oppression and exploitation.

其　五

日观东北倾，
两崖夹双石。
海水落眼前，
天光遥空碧。
千峰争攒聚，
万壑绝凌历。
缅彼鹤上仙，
去无云中迹。
长松入霄汉，
远望不盈尺。
山花异人间，
五月雪中白。
终当遇安期，
于此炼玉液。

No. 5

Mt. Sunview to northeast does lean;
Two cliffs stand with two stones between.
Seawater falls before my eyes;
Sunlight sways afar in the skies.
Thousands of peaks vie to be there;
Myriads of vales are void of air.
I recall him riding a crane;
No clouds now see his trace remain.
The tall pines reach the Milky Way;
They're a foot tall, seen far away.
The hill blossoms make a strange sight;

In the fifth moon they are snow white.
I'll meet the hermit anyhow;
I would make nectar with him now.

* Mt. Sunview: referring to the highest peak in the southeast of Mt. Arch, where one can see the sun rise from East Sea early in the morning, hence the name.
* crane: one of a family of large, long-necked, long-legged, heronlike birds allied to the rails, a symbol of integrity and longevity in Chinese culture, only second to the phoenix in cultural importance.
* the Milky Way: a luminous band circling the heavens composed of stars and nebulae; the Galaxy.
* nectar: in Chinese and Greek mythologies, the drink of the gods or fairies, and in botany, the saccharine substance secreted by some plants and forming the base of natural honey.

其 六

朝饮王母池，
暝投天门关。
独抱绿绮琴，
夜行青山间。
山明月露白，
夜静松风歇。
仙人游碧峰，
处处笙歌发。
寂静娱清辉，
玉真连翠微。
想象鸾凤舞，
飘飖龙虎衣。
扪天摘匏瓜，
恍惚不忆归。
举手弄清浅，
误攀织女机。
明晨坐相失，
但见五云飞。

No. 6

Morn sees me drink Queen Mother's Pool
And reach Heaven's Gate Pass at dusk cool.
Alone, my green lute I hold tight,
And walk in the mountains at night.
The moon to the bright mountains shines;
The wind rests in the tranquil pines.
The immortal tours the green mound,

When the reed pipe tune rings around.
The calmness pleases the pure sheen;
The Word Temple links to the real green.
One can imagine phoenixes dance
And dragons and tigers there prance.
I'd pick up the gourds off the blue;
So entranced, I forget to go.
When I play with the Milky Way,
The Weaver's loom I disarray.
At dawn, all these scenes will be gone,
Only five-colored clouds fly on.

* Queen Mother's Pool: referring to Jade Pool, a fairy pool on Mt. Queen, by which Mother West holds banquets.
* Heaven's Gate Pass: Heaven's Gate. There are three Heaven's Gates on Mt. Arch: First Heaven's Gate, Middle Heaven's Gate, and South Heaven's Gate.
* the Word Temple: referring to all Wordist temples on Mt. Arch.
* the Weaver: referring to a Vega. In Chinese mythology, Lady Weaver is the daughter of Jade Emperor, living in the east of the Milky Way and good at weaving with clouds. As is told, she stole out of the sky and fell in love with poor cowherd and they gave birth to two children. When found, Weaver Maid was taken away and kept away from the cowherd by Queen Mother, who made the Silver River (the Milky Way) with her hair pin. They could only meet once a year by crossing the bridge made for them by magpies.

秋夜与刘砀山泛宴喜亭池

明宰试舟楫，
张灯宴华池。
文招梁苑客，
歌动郢中儿。
月色望不尽，
空天交相宜。
令人欲泛海，
只待长风吹。

Attending a Feast with Fan Liu, Magistrate of Tangshan, at Glee Kiosk Pool on an Autumn Night

I try the oar with Magistrate;
At the clear pool we've a feast great.
Liang verse we chant is of the best;
Ying songs they sing can all arrest.
Boundless is the light of the moon;
The sky can everything attune.
Across the ocean I would sail,
And expect a high wind to hail.

* Liang: referring to Liang's Park, also called Prince Liang's Park, a large royal park established by Prince Piety of Liang in the Western Han dynasty, about 150 kilometers in circumference, built on the ruins of the State of Sung, that is, today's Shangch'iu, Honan Province, the birthplace of Sir Lush, one of the forerunners of Wordism.

* Ying: the capital of the State of Ch'u in the Eastern Chough dynasty, and an alternative name for the lands in present-day Hupei and northern Hunan.
* The sky can everything attune: The sky or the Heaven has been personalized and regarded as the supreme sovereign of the universe since the beginning of Chinese history.

携妓登梁王栖霞山孟氏桃园中

碧草已满地，
柳与梅争春。
谢公自有东山妓，
金屏笑坐如花人。
今日非昨日，
明日还复来。
白发对绿酒，
强歌心已摧。
君不见梁王池上月，
昔照梁王樽酒中。
梁王已去明月在，
黄鹂愁醉啼春风。
分明感激眼前事，
莫惜醉卧桃园东。

Climbing Mt. Perching Clouds of Prince Liang with Courtesans and Entering Meng's Peach Orchard

Green grass spreads all over the ground;
Willows and plums vie, to vie all-round.
Lord Glee's courtesans on the East Hill;
By the screen they smile, charm to spill.
Today is not yesterday, nay;
Tomorrow will come, on the way.
My white hair faces the green wine;

I try to sing, only to whine.
Don't you espy the moon o'er Prince Liang's pool, high up
Just like today once shone to his whine cup.
Prince Liang is now gone, the moon still on high;
The orioles sad and drunk to spring wind cry.
I, perturbed by what is before me,
Lie east of Peach Orchard, so drunk, so free.

* Prince Liang: Prince Piety of Liang in the Western Han dynasty, Emperor Civil's second official son, Emperor Scene's younger brother.
* Lord Glee: the court title of Lingyün Hsieh (A.D. 385 – A.D. 433), a highborn poet, Buddhist, traveler, famous for landscape poems, and a famous mountain climber, who invented special mountain shoes.
* The East Hill: the East Hills, located in Shaohsing, a place for reclusion, where An Hsieh (A.D. 320 – A.D. 385) used to live.

与从侄杭州刺史良游天竺寺

挂席凌蓬丘，
观涛憩樟楼。
三山动逸兴，
五马同遨游。
天竺森在眼，
松风飒惊秋。
览云测变化，
弄水穷清幽。
叠嶂隔遥海，
当轩写归流。
诗成傲云月，
佳趣满吴洲。

Touring Heaven Bamboo Temple with Liang, My Cousin, Governor of Hangchow

To tour Thistle Knoll we now row;
Atop Camphor Tower tides we'll view.
The three mountains boost up my glee;
The five horses gallop with me.
Heaven Bamboo's under my eyes;
The autumn sough does pines surprise.
Watching the clouds, we see all change;
Playing the flow, far we can range.
The great sea is beyond the height;
At door, about the flow I write.

No sun or moon, the verse is done;
In Wu we've much pleasure and fun.

* Hangchow: the capital of present-day Chechiang Province.
* Thistle Knoll: referring to Mt. P'englai, one of the three fairy mountains on the East Sea.
* Camphor Tower: Camphor Tower Post, on the bank of the Ch'ient'ang River.
* the three mountains: referring to the three fairy hills floating on East Sea, that is, present-day China East Sea.
* the five horses: indicating a magistrate. In ancient times, magistrates were once allowed to ride a cart driven by five horses.
* Heaven Bamboo: referring to a Buddhist temple by West Lake.

同友人舟行游台越作

楚臣伤江枫，
谢客拾海月。
怀沙去潇湘，
挂席泛冥渤。
蹇予访前迹，
独往造穷发。
古人不可攀，
去若浮云没。
愿言弄倒景，
从此炼真骨。
华顶窥绝冥，
蓬壶望超忽。
不知青春度，
但怪绿芳歇。
空持钓鳌心，
从此谢魏阙。

Cruising T'aiyüeh with My Friend

Yüan did river maples deplore;
Hsieh would pick the moon at seashore.
Yüan sank in the stream with a stone;
Hsieh sailed across the sea alone.
Poor, I run where forebears have run,
And row to the coast, a lonely one.
Ancients I have no chance to see;

Like clouds they float and nowhere be.
A shadow upside down I'd play;
Be an immortal man I may.
Atop the peak I o'erlook the blue;
The fairy isle is vague but true.
I don't know how time flies away
But hate green and red fast decay.
To fish for turtles I've the mind
And thereby throw the court behind.

* T'aiyüeh: referring to an area covering present-day T'aichow and Yüehchow, Chechiang Province.
* maple: any of a large genus (*Acer*) of deciduous trees of the north temperate zone, with opposite leaves that turn red in autumn and a fruit of two joined samaras, a symbol of cordial love and good luck because of its bright fiery color.
* Yüan: referring to Yüan Ch'ü (340 B.C.- 278 B.C.), a great patriotic poet and official of Ch'u, who sank himself with a stone into the River Milo, so aggrieved at his broken state.
* Hsieh: referring to Lingyün Hsieh (A.D. 385 - A.D. 433), a highborn poet, idyllist, Buddhist and traveler, famous for landscape poems.

下终南山过斛斯山人宿置酒

暮从碧山下,
山月随人归。
却顾所来径,
苍苍横翠微。
相携及田家,
童稚开荆扉。
绿竹入幽径,
青萝拂行衣。
欢言得所憩,
美酒聊共挥。
长歌吟松风,
曲尽河星稀。
我醉君复乐,
陶然共忘机。

Descending the South Mountains to Drink with Ssu Hu, a Hermit

The dusk leaves the mountains behind;
The moon does rise to follow me.
Turning back, I see the path wind
And the green turn dim, dark to be.
His hand in mine, we near his farm;
His kid opens the bramble door.
The bamboos lead to a place calm;
The vines pull my cloak, not looked for.

It's a place to talk, laugh and rest,
And we drink for a roundelay.
We sing *Wind thru Pines*, as if blessed
Until stars leave the Milky Way.
I reel drunk and once more you smile
And we both laugh at the world's guile.

* the South Mountains: one of the mountains of Ch'in Ridge, where dwelt many hermits, located to the south of Long Peace, Sha'anhsi Province. It is the birthplace of Wordist culture, Buddhist culture, Filial Piety culture, Longevity culture, Bellheads culture and Plutus culture and is praised as the Capital of Fairies, the crown of Heavenly Abode and the Promised Land of the World.
* the moon: the celestial body that revolves around the earth from west to east, which appears at night and gives off shining silvery light, an image of purity and solitude in Chinese culture.
* bramble door: a door made of brambles, a symbol of country life.
* bamboo: a tall, tree-like or shrubby grass in tropical and semi-tropical regions, a symbol of integrity and altitude, one of the four most important images in Chinese literature, which are wintersweet, orchid, bamboo, and chrysanthemum.
* *Wind thru Pines*: an ancient Chinese song and an old Chinese zither tune.
* the Milky Way: the Silver River in Chinese mythology in contrast with Greek mythology relevant to Zeus and Hera. Physically, it is a luminous band circling the heavens composed of stars and nebulae; the Galaxy.

朝下过卢郎中叙旧游

君登金华省，
我入银台门。
幸遇圣明主，
俱承云雨恩。
复此休浣时，
闲为畴昔言。
却话山海事，
宛然林壑存。
明湖思晓月，
叠嶂忆清猿。
何由返初服，
田野醉芳樽。

A Talk of the Past with Lu, the Royal Guard, After the Levee

You ascend to Gold Flora Board,
And I enter Silver Mound Gate.
You have met with a divine lord,
And I've His Majesty's grace great.
Again, we have a rest today;
We may talk of the past now free.
Then uphill or seaside we did play;
The scenery is still fresh to me.
On Lake Light we played, the moon fair;
On the hills monkeys cried and reeled.

When can we go back to stroll there?
Or we may lie drunk in the field.

* levee: a morning reception or an assembly at the court of a sovereign or at the house of a great personage. In ancient China, a levee at court was held every five days.
* Gold Flora Board: a Han palace, referring to Undergate Department in the T'ang dynasty.
* Silver Mound Gate: indicating the imperial academy located next to the Silver Mound Gate.
* Lake Light: unidentified, probably a lake in the palace.

侍从游宿温泉宫作

羽林十二将，
罗列应星文。
霜仗悬秋月，
霓旌卷夜云。
严更千户肃，
清乐九天闻。
日出瞻佳气，
葱葱绕圣君。

Escorting the Lord to Hot Spring Palace

The twelve guard generals you find
Like the constellation aligned.
Their mails look like the chill moon bright,
Or like flags furling clouds at night.
All households quiet before sunrise;
The court music rings to the skies.
The daybreak welcomes the warm sun;
Around the Lord bliss has begun.

* Hot Spring Palace: 19 kilometers south of Greater Wild Goose Pagoda in today's Hsi-an, Sha'anhsi Province, a famous resort in the T'ang dynasty, still in service today.
* the twelve guard generals: escort guard generals.

邯郸南亭观妓

歌鼓燕赵儿,
魏姝弄鸣丝。
粉色艳日彩,
舞袖拂花枝。
把酒顾美人,
请歌邯郸词。
清筝何缭绕,
度曲绿云垂。
平原君安在?
科斗生古池。
座客三千人,
于今知有谁?
我辈不作乐,
但为后代悲。

Watching Playgirls at South Pavilion in Hantan

The Yan-Chao girls dance and sing best;
The Way belle players the lute play.
Like sunlight they're brilliantly dressed;
Their sleeves waved, all charm they display.
I look at the belle, holding my cup:
Can you sing me the Hantan verse?
The pure *cheng* tune rings on and up;
The beautiful voice the clouds stirs.

Where's Prince of Peace, the gallant one?
His old pool with tadpoles does teem;
He had three thousand hangers-on;
Today who is still in the team?
If we do not make merry here,
Our offspring at us fools will sneer.

* Yan-Chao: referring to northern areas of China, the place once belonging to the State of Yan and the State of Chao.
* Way: the State of Way (403 B.C.- 225 B.C.), a vassal state of Chough, one of the Seven Powers in the Warring States period.
* Hantan: the capital of the State of Chao in the Eastern Chough dynasty.
* *cheng*: an ancient musical instrument with thirteen strings in the T'ang dynasty and twenty-one strings at present.
* Prince of Peace: referring to Lord Plain of Chao, one of the Four Childes in the Warring States period.

春日游罗敷潭

行歌入谷口，
路尽无人跻。
攀崖度绝壑，
弄水寻回溪。
云从石上起，
客到花间迷。
淹留未尽兴，
日落群峰西。

Touring La Phu Abyss on a Spring Day

While singing I enter the vale,
Going, going, I reach the end.
I climb the cliff and cross the dale
And follow the stream to the bend.
Out of the boulders clouds appear;
The blossoms here do me arrest.
Unsatisfied, I linger here;
The peaks are in afterglow dressed.

* La Phu: an attractive mountain in today's Kuangtung Province, where Surge Ko, a hermit in the Chin dynasty, used to live in seclusion.

春陪商州裴使君游石娥溪

裴公有仙标,
拔俗数千丈。
澹荡沧洲云,
飘飖紫霞想。
剖竹商洛间,
政成心已闲。
萧条出世表,
冥寂闭玄关。
我来属芳节,
解榻时相悦。
褰帷对云峰,
扬袂指松雪。
暂出东城边,
遂游西岩前。
横天耸翠壁,
喷壑鸣红泉。
寻幽殊未歇,
爱此春光发。
溪傍饶名花,
石上有好月。
命驾归去来,
露华生翠苔。
淹留惜将晚,
复听清猿哀。
清猿断人肠,
游子思故乡。
明发首东路,

此欢焉可忘。

Accompanying Lord P'ei, a Civil Governor from Shangchow on a Tour to the Stone Maid Stream

Lord P'ei, you've an immortal air,
Kept far away from vain affair.
Looking like clouds o'er Blue Shoal,
You chase air purple with your soul.
As a governor of Shangchow,
You've done your best, so free of woe.
O'er the dust world you highly soar,
Or contemplate behind your door.
When I came here, you were in prime;
We talked in bed for a good time.
Screen furled, the peaks face me and you;
Sleeves waved, we point to the pine snow.
Now from the east town we come out;
And the west rock we stroll about.
The crags to the sky seem to soar;
The spring from the hill does down pour.
To the recesses we go on,
While lit up by the warm spring sun.
Blooms burst on the banks of the stream;
The stone enjoys the moon's pure beam.
Now you ask your groom so to go,
The green moss wet with heavy dew.
We linger there till night falls, dark;
The monkeys shriek again, now hark!

The shriek does me in sadness drown;
A vagrant, now I miss my town.
Tomorrow, I'll be on my way;
How could I forget our best day?

* Blue Shoal: an ancient town near Rising Bay in today's Hopei Province.
* Shangchow: the former State of Shang, a shire in the T'ang dynasty, and a district in present-day Shanglo, Sha'anhsi Province.
* moss: a tiny, delicate green bryophytic plant growing on damp decaying wood, wet ground, humid rocks or trees, producing capsules which open by an operculum and contain spores. Under a poet's writing brush, it may arouse a poetic feeling or imagination.

陪从祖济南太守泛鹊山湖三首

Accompanying My Granduncle, Magistrate of Chinan, Boating on Lake Magpie, Three Poems

其 一

初谓鹊山近，
宁知湖水遥？
此行殊访戴，
自可缓归桡。

No. 1

You said Lake Magpie is so near;
But it turns out too far, you know.
Unlike Wang's call on Tai that year,
Now back home, we can slowly row.

* Lake Magpie: a lake surrounding Mt. Magpie, where the renowned physician Magpie (407 B.C.- 310 B.C.) in the Spring and Autumn period was buried, hence the name.
* Wang: referring to Huichih Wang (A.D. 338 - A.D. 386), a renowned calligrapher with a carefree attitude in the Eastern Chin dynasty, Tsu-yu by courtesy name. He once took a boat to visit his friend on a whim on a winter evening, and returned without seeing him for Hui already felt contented on the way.
* Tai: referring to K'ui Tai (A.D. 326 - A.D. 396), an artist in the Eastern Chin, and a friend of Huichih Wang's.

其 二

湖阔数千里，
湖光摇碧山。
湖西正有月，
独送李膺还。

No. 2

The lake is thousands of miles wide;
The lake light shakes the mountainside.
West of the lake up hangs the moon;
I can see you back very soon.

* the lake: referring to Lake Magpie, a lake surrounding Mt. Magpie, near today's Chinan, Shantung Province.
* the moon: the planet of the earth, which appears at night and gives off shining silvery light, an image of purity and solitude in Chinese culture.

其 三

水入北湖去，
舟从南浦回。
遥看鹊山转，
却似送人来。

No. 3

To North Lake the water does flow;
From Southern Moor the boat we row.
Afar, Mt. Magpie turns around,
As if to see us for home bound.

* North Lake: one of the lakes under Mt. Magpie.
* Southern Moor: south of Mt. Magpie and Lake Magpie.
* Mt. Magpie: a mountain where the renowned physician Magpie was buried, hence the name, near the north bank of the Yellow River.

春日陪杨江宁及诸官宴北湖感古作

昔闻颜光禄，
攀龙宴京湖。
楼船入天镜，
帐殿开云衢。
君王歌大风，
如乐丰沛都。
延年献佳作，
邈与诗人俱。
我来不及此，
独立钟山孤。
杨宰穆清风，
芳声腾海隅。
英僚满四座，
粲若琼林敷。
鹢首弄倒景，
峨眉缀明珠。
新弦采梨园，
古舞娇吴歈。
曲度绕云汉，
听者皆欢娱。
鸡栖何嘈嘈，
沿月沸笙竽。
古之帝宫苑，
今乃人樵苏。
感此劝一觞，
愿君覆瓢壶。
荣盛当作乐，

无令后贤吁。

Accompanying Magistrate Yang of Riverpeace and Other Officials at Feast on North Lake While Reminiscing the Past

Once a Light Pay called Yan, I hear,
To woo the court held a feast here.
The tower ship cruised Lake Mirror glare!
The tent scraped the cloud thoroughfare.
There sung was *Great Wind* of the crown,
Like merry-making in P'ei Town.
Light Pay Yan read out his verse book;
Much like a great poet he did look.
I could not compare with him well;
He was prominent like Mt. Bell.
Magistrate Yang, you're cool and free;
Your name resounds high on East Sea.
Your peers are talents, all around,
Like jadeite trees that stroke the mound.
The bird-like boat casts a shade there;
The singing girls wear pearls so rare.
New tunes of the band all appease;
Old dance and soft voice each one please.
A song may move the Milky Way;
The audience's spellbound to the play.
Tic-tac, bit-bat, loud is the tune;
Lute, flute, the music drowns the moon.
There was a palace here, alas;

Today people come to cut grass.
At this one may be moved a lot;
Do drink, why not drink up your pot.
Go merry while we've glory plus;
Don't let our offspring laugh at us.

* Light Pay: referring to a senior position in charge of palace affairs.
* Yan: referring to Yanchih Yan (A.D. 384 – A.D. 456), Yannien by courtesy name, and a litterateur from Sung (A.D. 420 – A.D. 479) in the Southern dynasties.
* Lake Mirror: a large reservoir built in the Han dynasty, higher than the fields and the fields higher than the sea, 155 kilometers in circumference.
* *Great Wind*: an ancient song written by Pang Liu, the founding emperor of Han.
* P'ei Town: the birthplace of Pang Liu, located in present-day Hsuchow, Chiangsu.
* Mt. Bell: located in the east of Gold Hill in present-day Nanking.
* East Sea: East China Sea today, with an area of 770 thousand square kilometers.
* pearl: a smooth, lustrous, usually white and bluish-gray, calcareous concretion deposited in layers around a central nucleus in the shells of various mollusks or oysters, and largely used as a gem, medicine or given as a gift, a metaphor for the dearest one, a representation of nobility, purity and dignity in Chinese culture.
* the Milky Way: a luminous band circling the heavens composed of stars and nebulae; the Galaxy.

宴郑参卿山池

尔恐碧草晚，
我畏朱颜移。
愁看杨花飞，
置酒正相宜。
歌声送落日，
舞影回清池。
今夕不尽杯，
留欢更邀谁！

Inviting Cheng, Chief of Staff, to a Feast

The grass will dry, you are afraid;
I fear my complexion's decayed.
I'm sad to see catkins fly up;
It's the best time to drink a cup.
Let's see off the sun with our voice,
And by the pool dance to rejoice.
If we do not drink all tonight,
Who else to cheer can we invite?

* catkin: a deciduous scaly spike of flowers, as in the willow, an image of helpless drifting or wandering in Chinese literature.

游谢氏山亭

沦老卧江海，
再欢天地清。
病闲久寂寞，
岁物徒芬荣。
借君西池游，
聊以散我情。
扫雪松下去，
扪萝石道行。
谢公池塘上，
春草飒已生。
花枝拂人来，
山鸟向我鸣。
田家有美酒，
落日与之倾。
醉罢弄归月，
遥欣稚子迎。

Touring Hsieh's Pavilion

So old and poor, I lie ashore;
Resurgent, it's so fresh once more.
As I've been ill, for e'er in gloom,
In vain now I see all things boom.
Can you lend me your west pool please
So that I'd swim and myself ease?
I will sweep snow from olden pines

And walk on the stone path near vines.
Now there, on Mister Hsieh's pond, lo,
Spring grass has been awake to grow.
The blooming sprays lash up to sweep;
The mountain birds woo me: cheep, cheep.
The farmer has prepared good wine
That we will drink up when we dine.
When drunk, the bright moon we will greet,
While hearing kids come here to meet.

* Mister Hsieh: referring to Lingyün Hsieh (A.D. 385 – A.D. 433), a highborn poet, Buddhist, idyllist, and traveler, famous for his landscape poems in particular.
* the moon: the celestial body that revolves around the earth from west to east, which appears at night and gives off shining silvery light, an image of purity and solitude in Chinese culture.

把 酒 问 月

青天有月来几时？
我今停杯一问之。
人攀明月不可得，
月行却与人相随。
皎如飞镜临丹阙，
绿烟灭尽清辉发。
但见宵从海上来，
宁知晓向云间没？
白兔捣药秋复春，
嫦娥孤栖与谁邻？
今人不见古时月，
今月曾经照古人。
古人今人若流水，
共看明月皆如此。
唯愿当歌对酒时，
月光长照金樽里。

Asking the Moon, Cup in Hand

When will you come, o Luna in the blue?
I lay down my cup and would fain ask you.
The bright moon is too high for me to scale;
Where'er I go, it follows without fail.
It's near to the palace like a mirror bright;
When mist is dispersed, it sheds pure light.
At night one sees from the sea it comes on;

At dawn where from amid clouds is it gone?
White Hare pestles herbs year in and year out;
Who does E'erfair live with, who is about?
People today can't see the moon of yore;
The moon today did light people before.
People before, people today, both flow;
As ever, they have seen the moon like so.
I wish we could but sing long to the wine,
Our golden cups filled with Luna's fair shine.

* Luna: the moon, an important image in Chinese literature or culture as it can give rise to many associations such as solitude and nostalgia on the one hand, and purity, brightness and happy reunions on the other. What is "moon" in Chinese has at least two hundred names, like Jade Mound (yaot'ai), Fair Lady (ch'anchüan), Jade Hare (yüt'u), White Hare (pait'u), Silver Hare (yint'u), Ice Hare (pingt'u), Gold Hare (chint'u), Hare Gleam (t'uhui), Laurel Soul (Kuip'o) and so on.
* White Hare: In Chinese myths, there is a hare on the moon pestling elixir.
* E'erfair: a goddess in Chinese legends who lives on the moon.

同族侄评事黯游昌禅师山池二首

Touring a Zen Master's Mountain Pool with My Nephew, An, a Reviewer, Two Poems

其 一

远公爱康乐，
为我开禅关。
萧然松石下，
何异清凉山。
花将色不染，
水与心俱闲。
一坐度小劫，
观空天地间。

No.1

So much did Lord Far love Lord Glee,
Hence a Zen fane for you and me.
Sough, sough o'er the boulders and trees,
What a cool mound blown by a breeze!
The flowers are not with colors dyed;
Water and heart are free and wide.
While we sit still, an aeon flies by,
Watching the void twixt earth and sky.

* Zen Master: a title for an honored Buddhist who practices Zen, a kind of performance of quietude in a form of meditation or contemplation. When Sanskrit jana was spread to China, it was translated as Zan or Zen for this kind of practice.
* Lord Far: a founder of White Lotus Society. According to *Biographies of Lotus*

Society's Sages, Lord Glee saw Lord Far on Mt Lodge and there they translated *Hannya* and grew white lotuses and founded an organization called White Lotus Society.
* Lord Glee: the court title of Lingyün Hsieh (A.D. 385 – A.D. 433), a highborn poet, Buddhist and traveler, famous for landscape poems, and a famous mountain climber, who invented special mountain shoes.

其 二

客来花雨际，
秋水落金池。
片石寒青锦，
疏杨挂绿丝。
高僧拂玉柄，
童子献霜梨。
惜去爱佳景，
烟萝欲暝时。

No. 2

I come in the season of flowers;
Now Gold Pool's full due to the showers.
On the rubbles cold green does shine;
The willows shoot out twigs so fine.
A Wordist waves a whisk of hair,
A child proffers a frosty pear.
I hate to go from the good sight,
While misty vines welcome the night.

* Gold Pool: The bed of a pool called Seven Treasures is spread with gold sand according to *Amitabha*.
* Wordist: a follower or practitioner of the Word, the creator and exterminator of all things. In the T'ang dynasty, an age of proselytism, while Confucianism remained the guiding principle of state and social morality, Wordism had gathered an incrustation of mythology and superstition and was fast winning a following of both the court and the common people. Laocius, the founder, was claimed by the reigning dynasty as its remote progenitor and was honored with an imperial title, Emperor Dark One.

金陵凤凰台置酒

置酒延落景,
金陵凤凰台。
长波写万古,
心与云俱开。
借问往昔时,
凤凰为谁来。
凤凰去已久,
正当今日回。
明君越羲轩,
天老坐三台。
豪士无所用,
弹弦醉金罍。
东风吹山花,
安可不尽杯?
六帝没幽草,
深宫冥绿苔。
置酒勿复道,
歌钟但相催。

Drinking on Phoenix Mound in Gold Hill

We drink to keep the sights around,
So staying here on Phoenix Mound.
The waves write the age as of yore;
Both clouds and our hearts highly soar.
May I ask those days long ago

For whom the phoenix came? You know?
It's been long since it went away;
It should fly back to us today.
Lord outdoes all saints in the past,
So the able hold their posts fast.
Talents today are just like junk;
They pluck the strings and oft get drunk.
As east wind blows to mountain flowers,
Why don't we drink to fill our hours?
The six emperors lie neath grass;
Their courts are wet with moss, alas.
Don't talk any more, drink your cup;
The bells urge us to hurry up.

* Phoenix Mound: a mound that phoenixes gather on, more than one kilometer from the town of Health Builder (Chienkang), i.e. today's Nanking.
* Gold Hill: referring to Nanking, one of the most well-known ancient cities in China, a strategic fort as a gateway to the sea, which has been the capital of Wu, Chin, and many other states or kingdoms, such as the six empires called Six Dynasties and has flourished immensely with increasing trade and travel.
* moss: a tiny, delicate green bryophytic plant growing on damp decaying wood, wet ground, humid rocks or trees, producing capsules which open by an operculum and contain spores. Under a poet's writing brush, it may stir up a poetic feeling or imagination.

秋浦清溪雪夜对酒，客有唱山鹧鸪者

披君貂襜褕，
对君白玉壶。
雪花酒上灭，
顿觉夜寒无。
客有桂阳至，
能吟山鹧鸪。
清风动窗竹，
越鸟起相呼。
持此足为乐，
何烦笙与竽。

Drinking Wine at Clear Creek in Autumn Shore on a Snowy Night, When a Guest Sings *Partridge*

I wear a mink fur coat from you
And drink wine from your jade pot white.
In wine goes off the flake of snow;
And cold does vanish from the night.
A guest now sings a *Partridge* verse,
Who has from Cassiashine come here.
His voice the window bamboo stirs,
And e'en the birds get up to cheer.
With this we can have enough glee;
No pipe or flute we need, don't we?

* *Partridge*: an ancient song or a genre of lyrics bearing this title. "Partridge" is a symbol of lovesickness in Chinese culture, as it utters a plaintive cry sounding like: "bro-bro, no-go-go".
* mink: a kind of precious fur which is soft, thick glossy, brown, from an amphibious, slender-bodied mammal called mink.
* jade pot: a pot in good quality, crystally bright, a pot usually alluding to the purity of the holder's heart.
* Cassiashine: a town located in present-day Ch'enchow, Hunan Province.

与周刚清溪玉镜潭宴别

康乐上官去,
永嘉游石门。
江亭有孤屿,
千载迹犹存。
我来游秋浦,
三入桃陂源。
千峰照积雪,
万壑尽啼猿。
兴与谢公合,
文因周子论。
扫崖去落叶,
席月开清樽。
溪当大楼南,
溪水正南奔。
回作玉镜潭,
澄明洗心魂。
此中得佳境,
可以绝嚣喧。
清夜方归来,
酣歌出平原。
别后经此地,
为余谢兰荪。

A Farewell Party for Kang Chou at Jade Mirror Pool in the Clear Stream

When Lord Glee was the magistrate,
I went there for fun at Stone Gate.
There loomed an arbor on Lone Isle;
A millennium is but a while!
I've come to Autumn Shore to play
And thrice to Peach Source made my way.
Snow-capped are all mountains and peaks;
All vales resound with monkeys' shrieks.
With Lord Glee I aspire to go
And will converse with Prince of Chough.
Off the crags dry leaves we sweep clean
And raise our cups to Luna's sheen.
The creek flows before the mansion,
And it flows south to the ocean.
The back flow makes a mirror pool,
Which can purify one's mind and soul.
At this sight here we can rejoice,
Away from the world, from the noise.
In the depth of night we go back
To the plain, singing on the track.
Later on, if this place you pass,
Remember me to that fresh grass.

---

* Jade Mirror Pool: an abyss on the Peach Slope in Autumn Shore, in today's Poolton, Anhui Province.

* Lord Glee: the court title of Lingyün Hsieh (A.D. 385 – A.D. 433), a highborn poet,

Buddhist and traveler, famous for landscape poems, and famous mountain climber, who invented special mountain shoes.
* Stone Gate: Mt. Stone Gate, a mountain in present-day Ch'ingt'ien, Chechiang Province.
* Lone Isle: an isle in the E'erfine (Yungchia) River, about one hundred meters long, 35 meters wide and having two peaks, in today's Wenchow, Chechiang Province.
* Autumn Shore: southwest of today's Kuich'ih County, Anhui Province, rich in silver and copper resources.
* Peach Source: Peace Blossom Source. According to Yüanming Tao's writing, a group of Ch'in people fled to Peach Blossom Source to keep away from the turbulent days, and the people and their offsprings had lived an idyllic and isolated life for 500 years before a fisherman of Chin stumbled into their village.
* Prince of Chough: the 4th son of King Civil, brother of King Martial. After King Martial died, the king was too young to reign, so Prince of Chough became a regent. During his regency, he put forward fundamental laws and regulations in various aspects, and improved the patriarchal rite-music system, the feudal system, and the well-farmland system.

游秋浦白笴陂二首

Touring White Arrow Slope in Autumn Shore, Two Poems

其 一

何处夜行好？
月明白笴陂。
山光摇积雪，
猿影挂寒枝。
但恐佳景晚，
小令归棹移。
人来有清兴，
及此有相思。

No. 1

Where is the best to go at night?
White Bamboo Dyke neath the moon bright.
The hills reflect the light of snow;
A monkey shades the cold twigs low.
Too late, we can't in all rejoice;
"Let's go home", I hear your low voice.
We have come here, so fresh and glad;
Now we turn our oar, a little sad.

---

* White Bamboo Dyke: 12.5 kilometers from Poolton (Ch'ihchow), in today's Anhui Province.

其 二

白笴夜长啸，

爽然溪谷寒。

鱼龙动陂水，

处处生波澜。

天借一明月，

飞来碧云端。

故乡不可见，

肠断正西看。

No. 2

On White Bamboo Dyke I do shout;

The vale at night is chilled throughout.

Dragons and fish are thrilled to wake;

Lo, here and there, giant waves they make.

I borrow the moon from the sky,

Which to the end of clouds does fly.

Beyond my reach is my hometown;

I look west for long with a frown.

* White Bamboo Dyke: a dyke about 12.5 kilometers from Poolton (Ch'ihchow), near Mt. Nine Flowers, in today's Anhui Province.

* the moon: the planet of the earth, which appears at night and gives off shining silvery light, an image of purity and solitude in Chinese culture.

宴陶家亭子

曲巷幽人宅，
高门大士家。
池开照胆镜，
林吐破颜花。
绿水藏春日，
青轩秘晚霞。
若闻弦管妙，
金谷不能夸。

A Feast at the T'ao's Pavilion

In the depth a hermit does dwell;
Big houses hold peers you can tell.
The pond is like a mirror's shine;
A forest cannot flowers confine.
The blue stream mirrors the spring sun;
The window frames the dusk begun.
Compared with the pipe a belle plays,
Gold Dale feasts are not worth a praise.

* Gold Dale: originally a creek located west of Loshine in present-day Honan Province, where Ch'ung Shih (A.D. 249 – A.D. 300), a rich litterateur in the Western Chin dynasty, built a park and often held feasts there.

在水军宴韦司马楼船观妓

摇曳帆在空,
清流顺归风。
诗因鼓吹发,
酒为剑歌雄。
对舞青楼妓,
双鬟白玉童。
行云且莫去,
留醉楚王宫。

Watching Courtesans Dancing at a Feast in a Tower Ship of the Navy Under General Wei

Up to the sky does bulge the sail;
The wind does o'er the waves prevail.
The verse is to the drumbeat sung;
The wine is to the swordplay flung.
With the courtesans we well dance;
With twin-bunned fairies we fast prance.
O running clouds, don't go away;
In the palace let's drink and stay.

* courtesans: In Chinese blue brothel culture, Chinese scholars and officials often visited blue brothels for literary or art recreational activities with a specific courtesan, who was good at singing, dancing and traditional Chinese arts such as zither playing, go playing, calligraphy and painting.

流夜郎至江夏,陪长史叔及薛明府宴兴德寺南阁

绀殿横江上,
青山落镜中。
岸回沙不尽,
日映水成空。
天乐流香阁,
莲舟飚晚风。
恭陪竹林宴,
留醉与陶公。

Accompanying My Uncle, Vice Inspector, and Magistrate Hsüeh at Feast in the Southern Hall of Virtue Raising Temple at Riversummer on My Way to Nightboy When I Am Exiled

On the river looms Dark Red Hall,
While green hills to the water fall.
The shore bends on, so calm the sand;
The sunlit waves forward expand.
The divine tune in the hall flows;
The even wind to the boat blows.
Thanks for your feast in the bamboo;
You toast to me as your friend true.

* Riversummer: an ancient town tracing back to 350 B.C. when Sha-e was established and was officially renamed Riversummer in A.D. 589, one of the three towns that constitutes Wuhan, now called Chianghsia District under Wuhan.
* Nightboy: once the biggest kingdom founded by southern barbarians in the southwest, which was a provincial malarial land to Han Chinese. When a Han envoy visited Nigthboy, the king asked: "Which is bigger, Nigthboy or Han?" This self-important question has been a laughing stock ever since. In 27 B.C., Nightboy was wiped out by Han and was made a county.
* Dark Red Hall: a Buddhist temple hall, referring to Virtue Raising Temple in this poem.

泛沔州城南郎官湖

张公多逸兴，
共泛沔城隅。
当时秋月好，
不减武昌都。
四座醉清光，
为欢古来无。
郎官爱此水，
因号郎官湖。
风流若未减，
名与此山俱。

Boating on Officials Lake South of Mien Town

A spruce air Mister Chang does show;
South of the town of Mien we row.
The autumn moon does rightly shine;
As bright as Mightboom Town is fine.
The guests are drunk, drunk all around;
No such fun before could be found.
The lake's loved by officials all;
Officials Lake this place they call.
If ne'er goes down your grace or power,
Your name like the mountains will tower.

* Officials Lake: a lake inside Hanshine, one of the three towns that make today's

Wuhan.
* Mien: referring to Hanshine, an ancient town and a district in present-day Wuhan, Hupei Province.
* the moon: the celestial body that revolves around the earth from west to east as a satellite, which appears at night and gives off shining silvery light, an image of purity and solitude in Chinese culture.
* Mightboom Town: Wuch'ang if transliterated, an important county in today's Hupei Province.

陪侍郎叔游洞庭醉后三首

Accompanying My Uncle, a Vice Minister, on a Visit to Lake Cavehall, After Being Drunk, Three Poems

其 一

今日竹林宴，
我家贤侍郎。
三杯容小阮，
醉后发清狂。

No. 1

We've a feast in bamboo today,
Like the Juan's, old uncle and lad.
Have three cups fewer the lad may;
Forgive me if I am drunk like mad.

* Lake Cavehall: a large lake in present-day Hunan Province.
* bamboo: a tall, tree-like or shrubby grass in tropical and semi-tropical regions, a symbol of integrity, fortitude and altitude. A Ching poet speaks of its character in a poem *Bamboo Rooted in the Rock*: "You bite the green hill and ne'er rest. / Roots in the broken crag, you grow, / And stand erect although hard pressed. / East, west, south, north, let the wind blow."
* the Juan's: referring to Chi Juan (A.D. 210 – A.D. 263), a poet in the Chin dynasty, and Hsien Juan, a renowned scholar and the nephew of Chi, both of them were among the Seven Sages of Bamboo Groves.

其 二

船上齐桡乐，
湖心泛月归。
白鸥闲不去，
争拂酒筵飞。

No. 2

We sing *Song of Oar* in the boat;
On the lake with moonlight we float.
The seagulls white do not off soar;
They fly o'er our feast and fly more.

* *Song of Oar*: a boatman's song, unrecorded in history.
* seagull: a kind of sea bird, any gull or large tern, a symbol of clean integrity. The seagulls in the Wordist book *Sir Line* (Liehtzu) are particularly sensitive to impurity of motive and will make friends only with the completely guileless and disinterested.

其 三

划却君山好，
平铺湘水流。
巴陵无限酒，
醉杀洞庭秋。

No. 3

I will blow Mt. Fair, will it blow;
So the Hsiang River can here flow.
I'll drink the Pa's Hill's boundless wine
To paint Cavehall's autumn, face mine.

* Mt. Fair: a mountain in the middle of Lake Cavehall, so named because the two fair ladies, i.e., Lord Mound's two daughters were buried there.
* the Hsiang River: a river in today's Hunan Province, the major source of Lake Cavehall.
* Pa's Hill: referring to Hillshine, present-day Yüehshine (Yüehyang).
* Cavehall: a big lake mainly in today's Hunan Province.

夜泛洞庭，寻裴侍御清酌

日晚湘水绿，
孤舟无端倪。
明湖涨秋月，
独泛巴陵西。
遇憩裴逸人，
岩居陵丹梯。
抱琴出深竹，
为我弹鹍鸡。
曲尽酒亦倾，
北窗醉如泥。
人生且行乐，
何必组与珪？

Rowing on Lake Cavehall to Find P'ei, the Royal Servant, for a Drink

The dusk falling, the Hsiang looks blue;
Downstream floats my lonely canoe.
The lake reflects Luna's bright glow;
West of Mt. Pa alone I row.
Immortal P'ei's place I pass by;
He lives on the Red Lift on high.
Out of the deep bamboo he comes;
Playing the lute, *Phoenix* he hums.
The tune o'er, my cup lies aground;
By the window, in mist I'm drowned.

Cheer up, go merry while we may;
Why worry about rank and pay?

* Lake Cavehall: a large lake in today's Hunan Province, with rich natural and cultural resources.
* the Hsiang: a river in Hunan Province, the major source of Lake Cavehall.
* Mt. Pa: an ancient name for Hillshine, present-day Yüehshine (Yüehyang), Hunan Province.
* P'ei: an immortal unidentified.
* the Red Lift: a red mountain that reaches high into clouds.

陪族叔刑部侍郎晔及中书贾舍人至游洞庭五首

Accompanying My Uncle, Yeh, Minister of Penalty, and Chih Chia, Scribe of Privy Council on Lake Cavehall, Five Poems

其 一

洞庭西望楚江分，
水尽南天不见云。
日落长沙秋色远，
不知何处吊湘君。

No. 1

West of Lake Cavehall, the Ch'u does divide;
Waves surge, no clouds in the southern skies wide.
The sun setting sees Long Sand's autumn fade;
To pay respects to Nymph, where can I wade?

* Lake Cavehall: a lake in today's Hunan Province, one of the biggest lakes in China.
* the Ch'u: the Ch'u River. The Min River joins Lake Cavehall and flows more than 150 kilometers to Land Sand Prefecture, and this part is called the Ch'u River.
* Long Sand: referring to Ch'angsha if transliterated, a vassal state in the Han dynasty, a prefecture in the T'ang dynasty and now the capital city of present-day Hunan Province.
* Nymph: referring to the goddess of the Hsiang River.

其 二

南湖秋水夜无烟，
耐可乘流直上天？
且就洞庭赊月色，
将船买酒白云边。

No. 2

The autumn's South Lake sees no mist at night,
We can ride the waves up to the sky, right?
I'd borrow from Lake Cavehall Luna's shine,
So I could row to white clouds to buy wine.

* South Lake: alias Lake Cavehall, so named because it is southwest of Yüehchow.
* Lake Cavehall: a large lake with an area of 2,740 square kilometers, a lake of strategic importance since ancient times, a place of many natural and cultural resources for today's Hunan Province.

其 三

洛阳才子谪湘川,
元礼同舟月下仙。
记得长安还欲笑,
不知何处是西天?

No. 3

Ee Chia, brilliant, was exiled to Hsiang here;
Ying Li, moonlit, canoed with his friend dear.
Did they miss the court? A laugh or a sigh?
Did they remember still the western sky?

* Ee Chia: Ee Chia (200 B.C.- 168 B.C.), a political commentator, litterateur, who gained his fame when he was young. When he served as an official, he was envied by those higher-ranking ministers. In 176 B.C., Chia was exiled to Long Sand.
* Hsiang: the southern area of China, mainly today's Hunan Province.
* Ying Li: Ying Li (A.D. 110 - A.D. 169), a renowned scholar in the Eastern Han dynasty. He had a high reputation. When his friend T'ai Kuo (A.D. 128 - A.D. 169), a scholar, left the capital, there were many people coming to see him off but Kuo left only with Ying Li.

其 四

洞庭湖西秋月辉，
潇湘江北早鸿飞。
醉客满船歌白苎，
不知霜露入秋衣。

No. 4

West of Lake Cavehall the moon sheds chill light;
North of the Hsiang wild geese to dawning flight.
The guests with their song *Ramie* fill their boat,
Not realizing frost's fallen on their coat.

* Lake Cavehall: a lake in today's Hunan Province.
* the moon: the planet of the earth, which appears at night and gives off shining silvery light, an image of purity and solitude in Chinese culture.
* the Hsiang: a river in today's Hunan Province, the major source of Lake Cavehall.
* *Ramie*: a folk song in Wu, which became a psalm later.
* wild goose: an undomesticated goose that is caring and responsible, taken as a symbol of benevolence, righteousness, good manner, wisdom, and faith in Chinese culture.

其 五

帝子潇湘去不还，
空馀秋草洞庭间。
淡扫明湖开玉镜，
丹青画出是君山。

No. 5

Hibiscus's wife from South Land went back,
And stayed on Cavehall in autumn grass slack.
She makes up to the mirror shining now;
Mt. Fair looms there as her well-painted brow.

* Hibiscus: Shun if transliterated, the Double-pupiled One, an ancient sovereign, a descendant of Lord Yellow and Lord Mound's son-in-law, regarded as one of Five Lords in prehistoric China.
* South Land: the area south of Lake Cavehall.
* Mt. Fair: a mountain in the middle of Lake Cavehall, so named because two fair ladies, Hibiscus's two wives, Fairgrand and Shebloom, were buried there.

楚江黄龙矶南宴杨执戟治楼

五月分五洲，
碧山对青楼。
故人杨执戟，
春赏楚江流。
一见醉漂月，
三杯歌棹讴。
桂枝攀不尽，
他日更相求。

Feasting with Yang South of Yellow Dragon Rocks near the Ch'u River

The fifth moon, I come to Five Shoals;
The blue tower faces the green knolls.
Old Yang his halberd did once play;
Now he's come to the Ch'u to stay.
We drink and to the moon we'd soar
Three cups drunk, we sing *Song of Oar*.
Don't care about your laurel spray;
Think of tomorrow thine next day.

* the Ch'u: the Ch'u River, flowing mainly in today's Hunan Province.
* Five Shoals: five shoals in a group in the Long River, hence called Five Shoals, between today's Huangchow and Chiangchow.
* *Song of Oar*: a boatman's song, probably a ballad or a folk song.
* laurel: laurus nobilis, an evergreen shrub with aromatic, lance-shaped leaves, yellowish flowers, and succulent, cherry-like fruit, a symbol of glory usually in the

form of a crown or wreath of laurel to indicate honor or high merit, especially when one had passed Grand Test, i.e. Civil Service Examinations for selecting government officials, in ancient China. In Chinese mythology, there is a colossal laurel tree that is more than 1,500 meters tall on the moon, and it would never fall even though Kang Wu, a banished immortal, has kept cutting it.

铜官山醉后绝句

我爱铜官乐，
千年未拟还。
要须回舞袖，
拂尽五松山。

A Quatrain After I'm Drunk at the Copper Hills

The Copper Hills I love so much;
I'd stay and keep to it as such.
My long sleeve I will throw around
To stroke all of the Five Pine Mound.

* the Copper Hills: located in present-day T'ungling, Anhui Province.
* the Five Pine Mound: located in T'ungling, Anhui Province.

与南陵常赞府游五松山

安石泛溟渤，
独啸长风还。
逸韵动海上，
高情出人间。
灵异可并迹，
澹然与世闲。
我来五松下，
置酒穷跻攀。
征古绝遗老，
因名五松山。
五松何清幽，
胜境美沃洲。
萧飒鸣洞壑，
终年风雨秋。
响入百泉去，
听如三峡流。
剪竹扫天花，
且从傲吏游。
龙堂若可憩，
吾欲归精修。

Touring Mt. Five Pines with Ch'ang, Magistrate of Southridge

There the blue cruised he, Steady Stone,
And rode a wind and hailed alone.

With grace he swerved, the sea was whirled,
And his sublime sight topped the world.
He sought aliens with altitude,
And viewed the world with solitude.
Now I arrive at Mt. Five Pines
And drink, and climb to all confines.
I ask the old and I ask all
Why people this mount Five Pines call.
Mt. Five Pines is a place so cool,
Much better than Mt. Fertile Shoal.
The cave vibrates, a soughing sound,
With chill winds and rains all year round.
A hundred springs with great noise splash,
Like Three Gorges flowing so rash.
I'll cut bamboo and sweep the sky,
And tour with proud ones far and nigh.
In Dragon Hall if I could rest,
I would practice and myself test.

* Southridge: Southridge County in today's Anhui Province, a gateway to Two Mountains and One Lake (Mt. Yellow, Mt. Nine Flowers, and Great Peace Lake), established as a county in A.D. 525 by Emperor Martial of Liang (A.D. 464 – A.D. 549) in the Southern Dynasties period.
* Mt. Five Pines: located in today's T'ungling, Anhui Province, so named because there grew five pines on the very top. According to *Geographical Wonders* compiled in the Southern Sung dynasty, "The mountain boasted old pines, five in one, a pentad, reaching high to the sky with scale-like bark on the trunk."
* Mt. Fertile Shoal: referring to Wochow if transliterated, Chechiang Province.
* Three Gorges: referring to three gorges of the Willow River in the west of Chechiang.
* Dragon Hall: a Buddhist temple on Mt. Five Pines.

宣 城 青 溪

青溪胜桐庐，
水木有佳色。
山貌日高古，
石容天倾侧。
彩鸟昔未名，
白猿初相识。
不见同怀人，
对之空叹息。

The Clear Brook in Hsuan

How wonderful is the Clear Brook?
Better than T'ung Lodge it does look.
The rocks are from the distant past;
The stones are from the welkin vast.
The colorful birds have no name;
The white apes each other acclaim.
I've no soul mates before my eyes;
I heave a long sigh to the skies.

* Hsuan: an ancient town in present-day Hsuan, Anhui Province, a county instituted in the early years of the Ch'in Emperor under the Prefecture of Redshine. It became a prefecture in 281 during the Chin dynasty. It is well known for rich historical legacies, and best remembered for its high-quality rice paper.
* T'ung Lodge: a county in present-day Chechiang Province.

与谢良辅游泾川陵岩寺

乘君素舸泛泾西，
宛似云门对若溪。
且从康乐寻山水，
何必东游入会稽。

Visiting Rock Temple by the Ching Stream with Liangfu Hsieh

The Ching Stream west sees me in your canoe,
Like by Cloud Gate, in the Joyeh I row.
I feel like touring with Lord Glee, well pleased;
Why should I climb Mt. Summit in the east?

* the Ching Stream: a stream in Hsuan.
* Cloud Gate: a Buddhist temple built in A.D. 407 in the Eastern Chin dynasty, in present-day Shaohsing, Chechiang Province.
* the Joyeh: a stream in the south of present-day Shaohsing, flowing into Lake Mirror, which is said to be the place where the belle West Maid did her laundry.
* Lord Glee: the title Lingyün Hsieh (A.D. 385 – A.D. 433) inherited from his grandfather. Hsieh, once the Prefect of Yungchia, was a highborn poet, Buddhist, idyllist and traveler, famous for landscape poems in particular.
* Mt. Summit: referring to the K'uaichi Mountains in present-day Chechiang Province, where Worm convened a summit attended by vassal lords, hence the name.

游水西简郑明府

天宫水西寺，
云锦照东郭。
清湍鸣回溪，
绿水绕飞阁。
凉风日潇洒，
幽客时憩泊。
五月思貂裘，
谓言秋霜落。
石萝引古蔓，
岸笋开新箨。
吟玩空复情，
相思尔佳作。
郑公诗人秀，
逸韵宏寥廓。
何当一来游，
惬我雪山诺。

Touring West Water to See Magistrate Cheng

West Water and Heaven Hall there,
The clouds o'er East Town seem to glare.
The whirlpools turn fast to resound;
The tower o'erlooks water around.
My face is caressed by a breeze;
The cool I enjoy, quite at ease.

Though it's May, I need marten fur;
Frost falls with wind and hears a whir.
The trailer leads out an old vine,
Bamboo shoots ashore, what a sign.
I would with the mountains converse,
And I think of you, your great verse.
Mister Cheng, what a poet you are!
Your grace and your voice flow afar.
Come and tour with me if you will,
My promise of Snow to fulfil.

* West Water and Heaven Hall: temples in Mt. West Water, 2.5 kilometers from Ching County, Hsuan, Anhui Province.
* marten: a weasel-like fur-bearing carnivorous animal (genus *Martes*) having arboreal habits as the pine marten and the large sturdy fisher marten; also the fur of a marten used for the making of expensive clothing.
* Snow: Mt. Snow, where Manjusri used to teach Buddhism.

九 日 登 山

渊明归去来,
不与世相逐。
为无杯中物,
遂偶本州牧。
因招白衣人,
笑酌黄花菊。
我来不得意,
虚过重阳时。
题舆何俊发,
遂结城南期。
筑土按响山,
俯临宛水湄。
胡人叫玉笛,
越女弹霜丝。
自作英王胄,
斯乐不可窥。
赤鲤涌琴高,
白龟道冯夷。
灵仙如仿佛,
奠酹遥相知。
古来登高人,
今复几人在?
沧洲违宿诺,
明日犹可待。
连山似惊波,
合沓出溟海。
扬袂挥四座,

酩酊安所知？
齐歌送清扬，
起舞乱参差。
宾随落叶散，
帽逐秋风吹。
别后登此台，
愿言长相思。

Climbing a Mountain on Double Ninth Day

By writing: "If I go, I go",
T'ao his retiring will did show.
Now in my cup I have no wine,
So with the governor I'll dine.
I think of Mister T'ao in white;
Drink? To daisies I'd him invite.
I do not feel quite well, alas;
Double Ninth Day I can't well pass.
Lord's inscription few can acquire;
I would south of the town retire.
I can build a shack on the hill
That can o'erlook the charming rill.
We hear the tune of the Hun flute
And the melody of the Yüeh lute.
E'en peers and all those in the court
Cannot have pleasures of this sort.
The red carp from the river leaps;
The white turtle for Riv'r God sweeps.
Those sprites can with you cheer up;
Cherish them and drink them a cup.

Of those who have climbed high of yore,
How many live, live as before?
Blue Shoal is not where you abide;
Morrow you can spread your wings wide.
The waves surge up like a mountain,
With cantos from the blue ocean.
When you toast to those guests around,
Who can reply if in wine drowned?
Some still drink, singing a Ch'i song;
Some still dance in a messy throng.
Like leaves dispersed, guests go away;
Their caps, wind-blown, overhead sway.
Some day this platform if you climb,
Remember here for our good time.

* Mister T'ao: referring to Poolbright T'ao (A.D. 352 - A.D. 427), Yüanming T'ao if transliterated, a verse writer, poet, and litterateur in the Chin dynasty, and the founder of Chinese idyllism, who was once the magistrate of P'engtse. T'ao resigned from his official post four times to live in seclusion.
* Double Ninth Day: There is a long tradition that people go climbing on this day, carrying chrysanthemums for their deceased dear ones and sprigs of cornel to exorcize evil spirits.
* carp: fresh water food fish (*Ciprinus carpiao*), originally of China, now widely distributed in Europe and America, a mascot in Chinese culture, symbolizing great success and harmony. An popular idiom "a carp jumping over the Dragon Gate" means climbing up the social ladder or succeeding in the imperial civil service examination.
* Blue Shoal: an ancient town near Rising Bay in today's Hopei Province.
* a Ch'i song: Ch'i's songs were usually characterized by seducing flippance, often to the accompaniment of music and dance with the same style.

九 日

今日云景好，
水绿秋山明。
携壶酌流霞，
搴菊泛寒荣。
地远松石古，
风扬弦管清。
窥觞照欢颜，
独笑还自倾。
落帽醉山月，
空歌怀友生。

The Ninth Day

Today, with clouds, it's a good sight,
The stream so blue, the hills so bright.
I have with me a pot of wine
And chrysanthemums cold but fine.
How old the pines and stones afar!
What happy band and strings they are!
I look into my cup: I'm fine.
Alone I laugh and then recline.
By wind my cap is blown away;
Where are you, friend, where are you, pray?

* the Ninth Day: referring to Double Ninth Day, the ninth day of the ninth moon in Chinese Lunar calendar. There is a long tradition that people climb a height and enjoy

chrysanthemums on this day to commemorate their ancestors.
* chrysanthemum: any of a genus of perennials (*Chryanthemum*) of the composite family, some cultivated varieties of which have large heads of showy flowers of various colors, a symbol of purity or longevity in Chinese culture.

九日龙山饮

九日龙山饮，
黄花笑逐臣。
醉看风落帽，
舞爱月留人。

Drinking on Mt. Dragon the Ninth Day

We drink on Dragon the ninth day;
The chrysanthemums at me sneer.
Drunk, I see my cap blown away;
The moon will keep me exiled here.

* Dragon: Mt. Dragon, a mountain in Tangt'u.
* the Ninth day: referring to Double Ninth Day, that is the ninth day of the ninth month of the year. It is a long tradition that families or friends gather, climb a mountain or a height and enjoy chrysanthemums on this day usually in memory of family members that have passed away.
* chrysanthemum: a genus of perennials with tha same name *Chryanthemum* in Latin, having large heads of showy flowers of various colors, a symbol of purity or longevity in Chinese culture.
* the moon: the celestial body that revolves around the earth from west to east as a satellite, which appears at night and gives off shining silvery light, an image of purity and solitude in Chinese culture.

九月十日即事

昨日登高罢，
今朝再举觞。
菊花何太苦，
遭此两重阳？

The Tenth Day of the Ninth Moon, an Observation

Yesterday the mound I climbed up;
Today again I raise my cup.
How sad the chrysanthemum sprays!
They've suffered two Double Ninth Days.

* two Double Ninth Days: Double Ninth Day is an autumn festival on the ninth day of the ninth month. It is a long tradition that people go climbing a height with chrysanthemums or dogwood on this day. The ancients usually held another banquet the next day after Double Ninth Day, so they picked chrysanthemums twice, hence two Double Ninth Days.
* chrysanthemum: any of a genus of perennials (*Chryanthemum*) of the composite family, some cultivated varieties of which have large heads of showy flowers of various colors, a symbol of chastity or longevity in Chinese culture.

陪族叔当涂宰游化城寺升公清风亭

化城若化出，
金榜天宫开。
疑是海上云，
飞空结楼台。
升公湖上秀，
粲然有辩才。
济人不利己，
立俗无嫌猜。
了见水中月，
青莲出尘埃。
闲居清风亭，
左右清风来。
当暑阴广殿，
太阳为徘徊。
茗酌待幽客，
珍盘荐雕梅。
飞文何洒落，
万象为之摧。
季父拥鸣琴，
德声布云雷。
虽游道林室，
亦举陶潜杯。
清乐动诸天，
长松自吟哀。
留欢若可尽，
劫石乃成灰。

Accompanying My Uncle, Magistrate of Tangt'u, Visiting Breeze Arbor at Transmigration Temple

Transmigration's to transmigrate,
Where Golden Roll's hung on the gate.
Is it nebula from the sea
That's caused the tower in air to be?
You're so brilliant on this lake blue,
Smiling, sparkling, a scholar true.
You help others with all your love,
With no suspicion, with grace above.
Like moonbeams in the water sway;
Like lotuses sprout out of clay.
In Breeze Arbor you sit at ease,
Enjoying an all-round fresh breeze.
And, you are in the shady hall;
The sun can only outside stall.
Your tea or wine there guests welcomes,
The wondrous plates full of carved plums.
A verse flies from your fluent hand;
All in nature you can command.
Uncle, the zither you play well;
Your virtues like thunder excel.
Sometimes in Wordist woods you stroll
And like T'ao drink up to your soul.
The melody pure moves the sky;
The pines in the wind sadly sigh.
If pleasure can come to an end,

Into dust one can a rock rend.

* Transmigration: a Buddhist temple.
* Golden Roll: a golden plaque hung on a wall or a gate.
* tea: an evergreen Asian shrub or small tree (*Thea sinensis*), having a compact head of leathery, toothed leaves and white or pink flowers. The cured leaves of this plant or an infusion of them are used as a beverage. There are four major types of tea in Chinese culture, namely black tea, green tea, dark tea and white tea, and a large variety of subtypes or brands. Tea, first cultivated in China about 4,700 years ago, is a household necessity, as is shown by an idiom: For a family seven things there need to be: firewood, rice, oil, salt, soya sauce, sugar and tea.
* wine: one of the most important beverages in Chinese culture, of which brown wine was brewed more than three thousand years ago and white wine (spirit) became popular in the Sung dynasty. Wine has an important position in Chinese life, such as literary creation, cultural activities, health care, cookery and so on.
* zither: a simple form of a stringed instrument, having a flat sounding board and from thirty to forty strings that are played by plucking with a plectrum. Zither, together with chess, calligraphy and painting are four skills that a traditional literateur is expected to master.
* Wordist: relating or derived from Wordism, which is predominantly naturalism. In the T'ang dynasty, an age of proselytism, while Confucianism remained the guiding principle of state and social morality, Wordism had gathered an incrustation of mythology and superstition and was fast winning a following of both the court and the common people. Laocius, the founder, was claimed by the reigning dynasty as its remote progenitor and was honored with an imperial title, Emperor Dark One.
* T'ao: referring to Poolbright T'ao (A.D. 352 - A.D. 427), a verse writer, poet and litterateur in the Chin dynasty, and the founder of Chinese idyllism, who was once the magistrate of P'engtse. T'ao resigned from his official post four times to live in seclusion.